ROBERTS & M/

CW00458137

THE A TOM WAGNER ADVENTURE
CHRONICLE OF THE
ROUND TABLE

Thriller

Translator: Edwin Miles / Copyeditor: Philip Yaeger

Imprint: Independently published / Paperback ISBN 9798491007622, Hardcover ISBN: 9798449090973

Cover Art by reinhardfenzl.com

Cover Art was created with photos from: depositphoto.com, nejron, Avesun, Kengssr_2017@hotmail.com, apattadis@gmail.com, udon10671, JITD, I_gorZh, Imaginechina-Tuchong, iStock: michalz86, zabelin, Scopio: Parisa Shahbazi

www.robertsmaclay.com

office@robertsmaclay.com

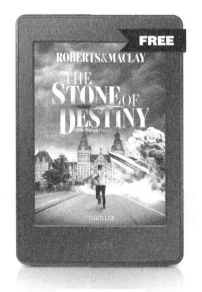

"The whole is greater than the sum of its parts"

Aristoteles

1

MOUNTAINS NORTHWEST OF KANDAHAR, AFGHANISTAN

THE THREE HUMVEES STRUGGLED UP THE BARREN, STONY mountain road toward the remote rendezvous point. The steep track pushed the military behemoths' V8 engines to their limits. The nine-man squads inside the front and rear vehicles were getting severely tossed around. The truck in the middle, however, carried only a single passenger, a civilian. Smartly dressed in a beige three-piece suit, he nevertheless wore a flak jacket and Kevlar helmet with protective goggles. He looked extremely out of place. Who was he? The soldiers didn't know. Their mission was to get him into the mountains and back in one piece, not to ask questions. When the job was done, they were to forget they'd ever seen him.

The men were not regular soldiers; they were private contractors. Mercenaries. Their job was to support US troops in crisis regions. But they didn't play by the same rules, and their style showed it. Instead of close-cropped military haircuts, some of them wore their hair long and had full beards, and beneath their flak jackets most wore nothing but a T-shirt and jeans. Some had even replaced their helmets with the *kufiyah*, the Arab headdress made famous by Palestinian leader Yasir Arafat in his day.

The snappily dressed man glanced at a portable GPS device. "Not far now," he said to his driver. He pointed ahead. "Just over this hill."

And so it was. Cresting the hill, they saw the shoddy buildings of a small village. In a clearing in the middle, a few kids kicked around a ball that looked as if they'd made it themselves. Horses ate from troughs or drank water in a small corral. At the sight of the Humvees, the women and children scattered like nocturnal creatures under a bright light, disappearing into their dilapidated houses. At the same time, the men emerged from those same houses. The Humvees were surrounded in seconds, the barrels of countless AK47s and even a few RPGs trained on them.

The vehicles rolled to a stop in a cloud of dust and the mercenaries leaped out and formed a perimeter. Crouching, they aimed back at the heavily armed locals. Two mercenaries manned the machine guns mounted atop the Hummers. Furious shouts echoed up and down the narrow valley.

Eyes wide and sweat beading on his forehead, the elegant man watched all this through the dusty windows of his vehicle, his fingers clenched around the GPS.

"We're here to talk to Omar Akhtar Akhundzada," the sergeant shouted in Pashto to the men, lifting his assault rifle—a Heckler & Koch G36K with a laser sight—over his head in a signal that they were not there to fight. The nervousness among the mercenaries grew as their sergeant stood facing the enemy. "Keep your heads, boys," the sergeant said to his men as they kept their rifles trained nervously on their adversaries.

One of the locals shouted a few words to his comrades, and the tension eased noticeably. After a short while, an elderly man with a long salt-and-pepper beard emerged from one of the houses. He wore a white turban and a traditional kaftan. The elegant man slowly opened the passenger door of his Hummer and climbed out. He edged cautiously through the ring of mercenaries and walked toward the elderly man, clearly the leader of this local unit. The Afghan's wrinkled skin was tanned dark brown by the sun. His remarkably friendly eyes looked out intensely from beneath bushy eyebrows, staring at his visitor. The elegant man stopped at a respectful distance.

"*As-salamu alaykum*," he said hesitantly.

"*Wa 'alaykumu s-salam*," the old man replied. Then, in perfect, British-accented English, he said, "Did you bring what I asked for?"

Probably studied at Oxford, the elegant man thought. *Nothing unusual about that.* "Yes," he replied, somewhat awed, and he raised his hands slowly into the air. Then, with great caution, he withdrew a small envelope from beneath his flak jacket and held it out to the leader. With a nod, the old man sent one of his men to fetch it. Then he opened the envelope and poured the two dozen small diamonds it contained into the palm of his hand. He nodded with satisfaction, and murmurs and cheers rippled through the ranks of his fighters.

He replaced the diamonds in the envelope and tucked it away inside his kaftan before shouting a few words to his men. Two of them ran some distance away, and the elegant man and the mercenaries watched as they lifted a trapdoor and climbed down. They reappeared a moment later, dragging a body into the daylight. It was a man, dressed in ragged clothes with a sack pulled over his head. He was feeble, hardly able to stand. His captors dragged his naked, filthy feet across the stony ground. When they reached the elegant man, they dropped the half-dead prisoner into the dust at his feet.

The Afghan leader waved contemptuously, ordering the newcomers to leave as he retired to his house. His fighters, however, did not move. They kept their guns on the mercenaries.

"Help me," the well-dressed man said, and he tried to lift the prisoner to his feet. Helped by one of the mercenaries, they carried the man, groaning in pain, to the cargo bed of the Hummer in the middle.

Maintaining their defensive positions to the last moment, the mercenaries retreated to the other vehicles. The convoy pulled out and disappeared behind the hill, heading back to base.

The elegant man turned back and looked at the man as one of the mercenaries pulled the sack off his head. The man nodded his thanks, then collapsed sideways and went limp. One of the mercenaries began treating his numerous injuries. The elegant man reached for his satellite phone and pressed a button.

"We've got him. Get the plane ready. We'll be at the airfield in two hours."

The three Humvees bumped back down the mountain road, trailing a billowing cloud of dust. Relief was inscribed on the faces of the mercenaries and the smartly dressed man. True, this was what they did for a living, but they all knew that this little outing could have had a very different outcome.

2

THOMAS MARIA WAGNER LOOKED DOWN FROM THE TOP OF the small hill and out over the sea. The rising sun glittered golden on the calm waters. His mount snorted, nostrils flaring, and champed at the bit.

"Easy, boy," Tom said gently. He stroked the majestic stallion's neck as it stamped restlessly on the spot. The sun rose slowly from the shimmering Mediterranean, and a cool breeze blew across the small volcanic island. Though it was midwinter, the island was so close to Africa that the temperature could reach the 70s even at this time of year. When the sun had risen fully and hung ablaze just above the horizon, Tom pulled the reins around and spurred the horse forward. He rode at a gallop along the steep, rocky coast until he reached his limit, quite literally: a ten-foot electric fence with surveillance cameras surrounded the estate where he was being held.

But his situation had definitely improved, and not only by comparison to the dark hole where he'd been left him to rot for weeks after being abducted. It was better than his regular home too, a houseboat in Vienna. After weeks of solitary existence in the dark, he'd woken one day in a soft bed on this island. The view was better, but he was clearly still a prisoner. The hermetically sealed estate was secured by high fences and countless gunmen guarded both him and the area.

Why was he here? Why wasn't he dead? What did they want from him? Questions and more questions, day in and day out. But for now, Tom had decided to do nothing and accept his fate, at least outwardly. He wanted to know why AF was going to all this trouble to keep him alive—Absolute Freedom, the global terrorist organization, never did anything without a good reason. Tom had made it his goal to destroy the network. AF was responsible, after all, for the death of his parents.

The only thing that really hurt was that he couldn't tell his friends that he was all right. Hellen would be sick with worry and Cloutard was probably scouring the world for him. But Tom was sure he would see them both again.

The luxurious estate had its own pool, and just before Tom reached the main building, he slowed the horse's gallop to a walk and turned toward the stables at the back. A woman in her mid-20s met Tom with a friendly smile.

"How was he this morning?" Sofia asked. The stable master's daughter had been his riding teacher for several weeks.

"Outstanding," Tom replied as he swung his leg over the horse's rump and dismounted. "I never thought I'd like riding a horse. But with one as magnificent as this, it's easy."

For a moment his mind returned to Hellen and their chance meeting almost a year earlier, months after they had separated. Horses had played a role there, too.

"You see, Signore, it is really not so difficult. You have come a long way."

"Thank you, Sofia." Tom handed her the Lipizzaner's reins and she led it back into the stable. He pulled his riding gloves off with his teeth, removed his helmet, and placed the gloves inside it.

"Sofia?" he called after her.

"Si, Signore?"

"When are you finally going to come with me? I'll go and get ready. Meet back here in ten minutes?"

"Oh, no, no, no, Signore. I am too young to die," she joked, and she gave Tom a radiant smile.

Pity, Tom thought. He turned away and went to the main building to get changed. A few minutes later, he set off along the path to the coast.

Sharp stones dug into the soles of his feet. His eyes were closed and the wind brushed at his face. A hundred feet below, waves crashed rhythmically onto the rocks. He enjoyed the deceptive peace of the moment, but it could not last forever. It was the calm before the storm. Tom opened his eyes and looked out over the endless sea. He simply could not get enough of this view. But the peace he felt came to an abrupt end when he saw something in the distance.

Focus, he said to himself. *You knew this day would come. You've waited for it.* The wind grew stronger and the crashing of the waves louder. He checked the zipper on his wetsuit one last time, then rotated his head until his neck cracked. He closed his eyes and took a deep breath in and out. Every muscle in his body tensed. He was ready. Without opening his eyes, he leaped forward with all his strength. Less than three seconds later, he slammed into the cold sea. It was not Acapulco, but it still gave him a kick. He was an adrenaline junkie, in his element when things were fast and dangerous. When his head broke the surface, he felt a rush of joy.

But it did not last long.

3

SOUTHERN FRANCE

THE LIGHTNING LS-218 RACED AT ALMOST 130 MPH ALONG the La Méridienne highway. The driver had just put the villages of Saint-Félix-de-l'Héras und Le Caylar behind him and now began to decelerate gradually. So far, he'd only been able to push the motorcycle to its top speed—just under 220 mph—once. The machine was a technical masterwork, and two things made it particularly special: it was the fastest production motorcycle in the world, and it was electric.

The rider exited the highway onto the D185. He was close to his destination, the little village of La Couvertoirade. He passed an old windmill and throttled back a little more. He rolled into the narrow streets of the medieval village, knowing that what he was there to do would not go unnoticed for long. La Couvertoirade was a tourist mecca. Its history fascinated people, not least due to the huge success of novels and films in recent years about the Knights Templar—and the conspiracy theories associated with them. The mass arrests of the Templars ordered by King Philip on Friday, October 13, 1307, were supposed to put an end to them once and for all—but they had only served to amplify the mythology.

The motorcyclist was one of the few people in the world who knew the truth of the legend, and it was very different than people had been led to believe.

He parked the motorcycle by a wall and dismounted. His leathers, boots, helmet and even the motorcycle were all in classic anthracite. They were nothing special to a casual glance, but close inspection revealed that they weren't just similar shades of gray, but identical. Achieving that visual harmony had cost a fortune.

He removed his helmet, unzipped his jacket and took a couple of deep breaths. It was pleasantly warm for the time of year, and yet he felt a breath of cool air as he climbed through the narrow alleys that led to the medieval fortress. About a hundred yards ahead, he saw his goal: a beige-colored building with dark brown shutters and a tiny balcony protruding over the front door, typical of the region. A small gray cat strolled across the cobblestones and stretched out on the step of the house marked *Mairie de la Couvertoirade*, enjoying the last of the day's sunshine. It meowed contentedly as the man approached the entrance, but a casual kick cleared it out of the way. The cat hissed and ran off.

The man's hand moved inside his jacket, checking, and he nodded to himself. Without knocking, careful not to touch the ancient handle, he pushed open the slightly open door with his foot and stepped inside.

He found himself in a small anteroom and looked off to the right into a study. The *Mairie* had been the village hall, but the population of La Couvertoirade had dwindled to less than two hundred inhabitants and it needed no formal administration. The old man in the study stood up from his desk at the sight of the unannounced visitor.

For several seconds, they stared at one another.

In a barely audible voice, the motorcyclist spoke two words:

"*Ynis Avalach.*"

The old man paled. So they had found him. He had chosen his hideout with care. No one would have suspected him of going underground in one of the best-known sites of the Knights Templar, and it had worked for years. Until today.

Any attempt to flee would be futile, he knew. He looked at the man in leather and could easily imagine why he'd been sent—many years ago, in another life, the old man had also been one of them.

Always searching. Always killing. Always hunting for the one clue that had eluded them. And when the old man had found that clue many years ago, he'd been faced with a decision. Share it with the Order or keep it to himself. He had chosen to say nothing and go into hiding. And for nearly fifty years he had stayed out of sight, undiscovered. But he had always known that they would find him eventually. And today, they had.

Because he had been one of them, he knew the art they had mastered.

As if in slow motion, the rider reached into his jacket and took out the weapon that the old man, unfortunately, knew all too well. It was the same one he himself had used countless times as a means to the Order's ends. To get what they were after, or to ensure silence.

He knew the shape of the dagger, modeled on the sword that had guided their every step, the sword of the man to whom they had sworn their unconditional loyalty, until death.

Now the day of his death had come. He would reveal the secret that he had kept all this time. No one could endure that kind of pain, and he had nothing to counter this weapon.

The old man nodded, resigned to his fate. He shared his secret with his executioner even before the rider had put the dagger to bloody use—and he asked him to finish the business quickly.

The motorcyclist acceded to the request out of respect for his former comrade, but not without a little regret: it meant that he would miss out on one of his favorite pastimes, and he had been looking forward to that the whole trip.

4

PANTELLERIA

A SPEEDBOAT WITH TWO MEN ON BOARD APPEARED ON THE horizon. Tom treaded water and watched as it roared closer. The motor dropped to an idle and the speedboat drifted directly toward him.

"Beavis, Butthead," he greeted the grim-looking men in the boat, two of his guards. "Nice of you to offer me a ride back to the beach, but I could swim it, too," he goaded. He knew perfectly well why they were there and, more importantly, who had sent them.

"Your presence has been requested," said Beavis, irritated. It was easy to see how much he'd love to break his cocky prisoner's nose, but he'd been forbidden from doing so by someone far above him in the food chain.

Over time, Tom had worked out how far he could push the guards, and had made a game out of trying to get under their skin. A bit of fun to pass the time. They only used actual force when he tried to escape in earnest, and then he ended up back in the dark hole.

With two strokes, Tom was at the starboard side of the boat. He reached out his hand and Butthead pulled him on board.

"Thanks, man." Tom clapped him on the shoulder, took a seat in the stern and put his feet up. He reached under his wetsuit, took out a pair of sunglasses, and put them on. Then he waved his hand regally, signaling to Beavis and Butthead to get the boat moving.

The two guards just shook their heads in annoyance. Beavis eased the throttle forward until the boat was shooting over the swells. When they rounded a rocky outcrop, there it was: the *Avalon*. Almost six hundred feet long and with five decks, the magnificent yacht was too big to dock in the harbor and had to anchor farther out. The waves thumped rhythmically against the bottom of the speedboat as it raced toward its mother ship. Beavis slowed the motor as they drew closer, and as if by magic, a huge hatch opened in the starboard side of the yacht's hull. Tom straightened up in amazement as the speedboat disappeared into the belly of the luxury yacht and the hatch closed behind them.

"Hello, Tom. Miss me?" said a female voice he knew only too well. Tom's mood took a 180-degree turn. From the shadows in the dimly lit docking bay stepped Ossana Ibori. She wore a skimpy white bikini, a stark contrast against her ebony skin. A translucent, ankle-length sarong wrapped around her hips completed the skimpy outfit. "I bet you can guess what's on my mind right now, can't you?"

Tom, unsmiling, pushed his sunglasses up the bridge of his nose with his outstretched middle finger.

Ossana was a killer, and she was one of the best. But Tom did not let her intimidate him. One day, he knew, he would enjoy wringing her neck. He wasn't a violent man and he avoided killing when he could, but he would happily make an exception for this woman. She was the epitome of evil.

Ossana held out her hand to help him out of the boat. Tom ignored her offer and tried to hop nimbly onto the dock. But the electronic ankle bracelet on his leg had become tangled in a rope and his landing was less then elegant. Ossana grinned and looked at his ankle.

"I hope that thing hasn't bothered you too much. A necessary measure, I'm afraid," she said with condescending good cheer. She snapped her fingers and one of the guards removed the device from Tom's leg. "But we won't be needing it now."

Ossana moved toward him until she was very close. She stroked his cheek tenderly, but Tom drew back in disgust. He would have loved to end this right there, but it would have been suicide to try. And he still didn't know what they wanted from him. But he knew the day would come when he would send the heartless woman to meet her maker.

Ossana's face turned serious again, disappointed at Tom's rejection. "Follow me," she snapped at him, turning around and moving toward the elevator that would take them to the higher decks.

5

VIENNA CENTRAL CEMETERY, AUSTRIA

HELLEN DE MEY RAISED HER HAND TO SHIELD HER TEARY eyes as she stepped out of the St. Charles Borromeo Cemetery Church. It was a beautiful day but it was cold, and the low winter sun blinded her.

She still could not grasp that Tom was dead.

For a moment, a memory flashed through her mind. She had met Tom when she was curator at Vienna's Museum of Fine Arts. He was a daredevil officer in the Cobra anti-terror unit, and just hours after they had met, they had set off across Europe in search of a treasure. And that first treasure hunt had been followed by a wild, intense, but short-lived love affair.

Lost in her thoughts, Hellen followed the pallbearers down the steps. François Cloutard was among them. Her path, Tom's, and that of Cloutard—a former criminal, smuggler and art forger—had crossed a year earlier. Cloutard had quickly switched his allegiance to the good side and he had been an invaluable member of the Blue Shield team, and a good friend, ever since.

Arthur Julius Prey, Tom's maternal grandfather, and Hellen's father Edward de Mey, who had only recently resurfaced, helped carry the coffin to its final resting place. Hellen held tightly to her mother's arm as the procession passed by the honor guard, a seemingly endless line of saluting police officers at the foot of the steps. Among them, Hellen recognized Captain Maierhofer, with whom Tom had always had a conflicted relationship. Even Chancellor Konstantin Lang, whose life Tom had once saved, was among the mourners, along with Vittoria Arcano and Maximilian Rupp, Tom's successor in the Blue Shield team. Mother Superior Lucrezia, whom Tom had met while passing through Italy, had come all the way from Rome to deliver a letter of condolence from the Pope and to pay her own respects in person.

"My sincere condolences," Hellen heard, but only distantly and dully in the back of her mind, as mourners passed one by one and offered their sympathies to her and Tom's grandfather. In his brief address, Colonel Maierhofer feigned great respect for his former protégé. "A tremendous loss for the entire police force," he said. But Hellen knew better. The blatant hypocrisy made her angry.

"Thank you, Tom Wagner. Without you, I wouldn't be here today. We will miss you. Austria will miss you." With these words, the Chancellor ended his heartfelt address. In his brief speech, he had outlined his unusual friendship with Tom and the gratitude and respect he felt toward him.

"Thank you for coming," Hellen said without turning around as Cloutard stepped up beside her. They stood apart from the funeral party, which was gradually dispersing.

"*Bien sûr, chérie.*" Cloutard passed Hellen his hip flask and they both drank a shot of Louis XIII to honor their fallen friend. For a few moments, they gazed into the distance in silence. Cloutard had spent the last few months searching for Tom and had only returned when news of his death arrived.

"What will you do now?" Cloutard asked, touching Hellen's shoulder gently.

"Papa and I are going to follow up a new clue. I have to get away from here and turn my mind to other things," Hellen said. "King Arthur," she added after a brief pause, and she smiled somewhat awkwardly. Cloutard seemed interested. "François, you must come with me. It wouldn't be the same without you. And I need people around me now for support." Hellen turned to her friend with a flicker of enthusiasm.

"*Excuse-moi, chérie.* I am sorry, but I need some time to myself. Now that your father is back, I feel like something of a fifth wheel. I do not want to stand in Theresia's—I mean your mother's—way."

Hellen nodded. She knew how he must feel.

"How are things with your father?" Cloutard asked.

Hellen's expression brightened a little. She glanced back over her shoulder to where Edward was standing with Theresia, Maierhofer, and the Mother Superior. Her father's recent return was the only good thing in her life. It had occurred to her that Tom had had to die so that she could get her father back, as if restoring a kind of cosmic balance . . . but no, she had to rid herself of that destructive, useless notion right away. She didn't want to think about the fact that just as she and Tom had been finding their way back to each other, fate had snatched him away.

At least she finally had closure. Not knowing what had happened the last few months had been unbearable. Not that anyone knew *exactly* what had happened—the news from the US that Tom had died in a secret undercover operation raised more questions than it answered.

"We're getting along very well, thank you for asking. It's as if he had never gone."

"What actually happened to him? Why did he disappear for almost twenty years?"

"He was a prisoner. Back then, he also worked for Blue Shield," Hellen explained. "During the Iraq war, he was there trying to protect cultural treasures, and was abducted. The other members of his team were all killed, and people assumed that he had been as well. He was rediscovered by accident by the US military during a mission, then spent six months in a hospital in Dubai." A small smile appeared on her lips. "And now he's come back to us. Come on, let's join the others," she said, and she hooked her arm into Cloutard's. Together, they strolled across the wide gravel courtyard to where the others were standing.

"Ah, Hellen," Edward said when they were close. "Sister Lucrezia has just told me that she has never been to the Palais des Papes in Avignon, so I've asked her to come with us."

Hellen nodded and shook Lucrezia's hand happily.

Theresia de Mey drew her daughter aside. "Are you sure you want to throw yourself straight back into work? Edward and Max can take care of this alone."

"Yes, Mother. This is what I need now. Don't worry. I'm happy that we're flying today."

"What about François? Is he going with you?" Theresia nodded toward Cloutard, who stood nearby with his mother, who had accompanied him to Vienna. At that moment, his phone rang. He raised his hand in apology and moved away from the group.

"No, and I'm sure you can imagine why." Abashed, Hellen cleared her throat.

"Well, then. The jet is ready. Max will meet you at the airport. Bring me back something nice for Blue Shield."

She paused for a moment and whispered in Hellen's ear as they hugged goodbye. "Let me know if you ever want to talk. About Tom or . . . your father."

Theresia watched her daughter with great concern as she climbed into Tom's old Mustang.

"You're worried about your daughter, aren't you?" said her assistant, Vittoria Arcano, who had observed the scene.

Theresia nodded wearily. "Yes. She has been through a lot. I hope it's not all too much for her." She breathed deeply and switched back to her usual businesslike self. "You'll take care of the matter in Istanbul?" she asked, looking at Vittoria.

Vittoria, surprised at the sudden change of subject, replied, "Of course. I'm as concerned as you about our two missing employees. I'm flying to Istanbul tomorrow evening to look into it."

"Do that. Report back to me as soon as you can," Theresia said woodenly. Her anxious mind was still with her daughter.

6

ABOARD THE YACHT AVALON, OFF THE COAST OF PANTELLERIA

"I'M GLAD YOU COULD MAKE IT, OLD FRIEND," NOAH Pollock greeted Tom when he left the elevator with Ossana and stepped onto the main deck.

"How could I turn down such a friendly invitation? And don't call me friend. We haven't been friends for a long time. And it looks to me like you've stumbled a couple of rungs up the career ladder."

The former Mossad agent stood at one of the luxury suite's large windows, gazing out at the futuristic helicopter parked on the helipad. Ossana crossed to the bar and began to mix some drinks. Tom remained standing close to the elevator and stared at Noah. He was not particularly surprised to see him here. In fact, he had reckoned with it. But to encounter him now, so soon after the death of his uncle—for which Tom held Noah partly responsible—called up a surprisingly deep hatred.

It was true: they had once been best friends, or so Tom had thought. They had fought on the same side, and

Noah had been seriously injured during a fateful mission. Until recently, he had been confined to a wheelchair. But it seemed that while he had regained his ability to walk, he had lost his humanity.

"Seems to me you got what you wanted," said Tom, nodding toward Noah.

"My legs, you mean? Yes, with the right contacts and enough money, many things are possible," Noah replied, sliding a hand over his upper leg.

"I hope it was worth it. A lot of good people suffered for it, and some even lost their lives," Tom said with barely contained fury.

Noah finally turned around and looked Tom in the eye.

"A small price in the grand scheme of things."

Tom's hand closed into a fist and for a moment he imagined leaping over the huge sofa and finishing off his "friend" where he stood. But Ossana had noticed Tom's inner struggle. Snakelike, she whipped a pistol out from under the bar and pointed it at him. Tom hesitated. *Not here, not today.* It took everything he had to stop himself from losing control. Tom had never believed he would be able to ever hate someone more than he hated his parents' killer. But here they were: Ossana Ibori and Noah Pollock.

Noah was about to go on, but Tom raised a hand and cut him off.

"Save your stories. You wanted to walk again, and there was literally nothing you wouldn't stoop to. You betrayed everything you once believed in."

Noah laughed. "Do you seriously think I've done all this just to walk again? Oh, yes, that was the icing on the cake, but this"—he swung his arms out theatrically and looked around—"this is so much bigger than either of us."

Tom moved slowly around the sofa and sat down. Ossana did not take her eyes off him. When Tom was sitting, she put the gun aside and picked up the drinks she'd just been mixing. She passed a glass to Noah and set a whiskey sour on the coffee table in front of Tom. It was his favorite drink, but he didn't even look at it.

"Exactly what made you think, even for a moment, that you knew me?" Noah asked, but Tom ignored the question.

"What the hell do you want from me, Noah? Why am I here?"

"Okay, fine with me, enough small talk."

Ossana went to a sideboard, picked up a remote control and pointed it at the wall behind Tom. She pressed a button and handed the remote to Noah. The windows darkened, and a panel slid to one side on the wall beside the elevator, revealing a huge monitor. When Tom turned and saw the picture on the screen, his heart almost stopped.

"Hellen," he said almost silently.

"Yes, there she is, your little girlfriend."

Tom jumped to his feet. "I swear, if you've—" But he got no further.

"Tom, Tom, take it easy. Hellen's fine and I have no intention of harming a single hair on her head." Noah pressed a button on the remote and the image zoomed out. Hellen was standing beside her mother, Cloutard, and a few other people Tom knew. They were standing outside a church. Then Tom saw the one person who should not have been there at all.

"Impossible," he whispered.

"Yeah, yeah. Time flies. Just accept it. Hellen's father has risen from the dead. And if you do exactly what I say, you can also return to the living."

Tom looked at Noah questioningly.

"Take a closer look. The picture was taken at Vienna Central Cemetery. At *your* funeral. With a little help from our friends at the White House, we've had you declared dead."

Tom sank back onto the sofa in disbelief.

"Here's the deal: Hellen's father is back, yes, but he won't be back for much longer if you don't help us."

"What's that supposed to mean? If I don't help you, you'll murder him?"

"Not at all. Why do you always have to think the worst of me? No, I want to help you save him. Mr. de Mey has resurfaced for one reason, and one reason only. He is suffering from a rare disease, and he doesn't have much longer to live. He's come back to spend the little time he has left with his daughter. Hellen, of course, doesn't know any of this, and she doesn't need to."

Speechless, Tom sat and stared at Noah as he paced back and forth in front of him.

"So, if you help us, you'll be saving two lives. Your own, and the life of Hellen's dear old dad." Noah took a sip of his drink, allowing his words to sink in. "As you can imagine, we have a number of outstanding scientists in our ranks. The same people who gave me back my legs can also save Hellen's father. What do you say?"

Tom thought it over for a moment, but it was a no-brainer. He wasn't going to let Hellen's father die, and at the moment he couldn't see another way out of his own situation. "I'm in. What do I have to do?"

"A wise decision. But then, you never were a *complete* idiot," Noah said, and he went to his desk and pushed a button the intercom. "Mr. Hagen, you can come in now."

Tom spun around as the door opened and Isaac Hagen entered the suite with an envelope in his hand. He moved around the sofa and, without a word, handed the envelope to Tom. The two men glared at each other like two pit bulls.

"Easy, you two," said Ossana. Tom took the envelope and Hagen stepped back.

"You'll find your exact instructions in there. Mr. Hagen here will coordinate everything else with you. Once you've brought me what I want, I give you my word that Mr. de Mey will be able to spend many more years with his daughter. Now if you'll excuse me, I have other things to take care of." Without waiting for an answer, Noah turned away and nodded to Ossana, who immediately led Tom and Hagen outside.

"I want regular updates," Ossana said to Tom as they climbed up to the helipad. "And behave yourselves, both of you. There is too much riding on this." She left them on the helipad and went back below deck.

"Go ahead. I still have to make a call," Hagen said.

Still somewhat uncertain, Tom crossed to the S-97 Raider helicopter. He slipped the documents out of the envelope and looked through them. *You can't be serious*, he thought. With a final glance back toward Noah's suite, he pushed the papers back into the envelope and climbed into the chopper.

7

VIENNA CENTRAL CEMETERY

"Allô?"

Cloutard immediately recognized the voice on the other end of the line. He'd made a deal with him, but so much had happened lately that he'd forgotten about it.

He instinctively looked around to make sure no one could overhear him, then moved a few steps away from the courtyard of the church, turning into one of the countless rows of graves. He listened in silence to what the man said, and what he heard made him forget everything around him. Suddenly, it didn't matter at all whether he'd said goodbye to Hellen and the others. His mind racing, Cloutard put more and more distance between himself and the funeral party, listening to the caller, his excitement growing with every step he took. His heart was pounding, and despite the chill and the wind whistling icily through the rows of graves, he felt a surge of warmth. With his free hand, he unbuttoned his black overcoat and loosened his tie.

"What do I have to do? Is there already a plan?"

His words were whispered, and his voice shook. He still could not believe what the caller had just told him. He sat down on one of the park benches scattered among the graves.

"A forgery? Yes, I have a few contacts there, of course, but until you called, other things were at the top of my priority list," he said.

As the caller spoke, Cloutard mentally reviewed his options, and his frown deepened. Regrettably, he had to admit that he did not have very many.

"*Alors*, before I decide, I am going to need more details," he said. He could not afford to pass up this opportunity. "Yes, meeting in person is always better for matters like this. You never know who is listening these days."

He got his feet again and hurried back to where the others were waiting. He had just arranged a meeting for the following day in one of the most beautiful buildings in the imperial city.

8

AVIGNON, FRANCE

THE BLUE SHIELD JET HAD LANDED ABOUT TWENTY minutes earlier at Avignon-Provence Airport. The airport was normally intended for domestic operations only, but UNESCO had secured them special approval to land.

Hellen had done some reading during the flight about the various legends surrounding King Arthur. The material was outside her area of expertise, really more her father's domain. He was the real Arthur expert, and she would learn a lot from him.

She should have been overjoyed, but again and again she was overcome by a wearying sadness. Did there always have to be a dark cloud in her life? For years, she had dreamed of doing research with her father, of experiencing history up close and personal, of making discoveries together. Of course, she had not been thinking of El Dorado, the Library of Alexandria, or the sunken city of Kitezh. All of those discoveries had come with Tom at her side. Now her father had reappeared, having fortunately survived his years of imprisonment in good shape. He had come back to her. And now Tom had been torn from the world, just when they were about to work things out again. She felt as if she'd fallen out of favor with fate.

"Personally, I think this mission is completely senseless. Thousands of tourists pass this way every day. What do you expect? That you'll press a few buttons, and a secret passage will open and suddenly you'll be holding King Arthur's diary? All you're doing is wasting taxpayer money."

Like Tom, Maximilian Rupp—Max for short—was a former Cobra. But that was the only thing they had in common. Max was an uptight flunkey, a drone unable to think for himself. Any ability he might once have had to think independently had been knocked out of him during his year in the Foreign Legion. His former Cobra superior, Captain Maierhofer, had played his part, too, stifling any last traces of individuality—a task Maierhofer had never achieved with Tom. Flexibility and creativity were foreign concepts to Max. Hellen had to smile when she recalled how Tom had once described his former colleague: "Stick a lump of coal up his ass, come back in a week, and you'll have a diamond."

After a few days, Hellen had given up trying to make Max understand her approach to their work. Together, Tom, Cloutard and Hellen had found a rhythm of their own, unorthodox but effective. They believed in something, and they found a way to get it. Hellen had learned that there were more secrets, treasures and mystical artifacts in the world than she had ever dreamed of. Max the

Minion would never understand that. Hellen was far from happy with her mother's decision. Again and again, she thought, *Replacing Tom with a dead weight like Max . . . it's unbelievable.*

True, she and her mother had grown closer in recent weeks, in large part because of her father's reappearance. That newfound affection had little to do with their new teammate, however. In fact, Hellen was peeved that Theresia had simply replaced Tom before they were even certain of his fate. She would hold that against her mother for a very long time.

Sister Lucrezia saw Hellen's inner turmoil and laid a consoling hand on her shoulder.

"Max, we have a job to do and we're going to do it," Edward de Mey said sternly. "Whatever it takes." He obviously knew how to deal with people like Max; the big man nodded crisply and went on loading their luggage into the rental car. The drive from the airport to the Palais des Papes in Avignon was uneventful, and half an hour later they were standing in front of the imposing medieval building.

"Wasn't spending a fortune to build St. Peter's Basilica enough? Why build a second papal palace? And weren't there once two popes at the same time? As if one wasn't enough." Max's tone was so arrogant and condescending that Sister Lucrezia almost forgot her manners and had to take a couple of deep breaths. Hellen had never seen the dignified woman so annoyed.

"The French king, Philip the Fair, set the project in motion," Hellen explained. "The Pope was chosen in

Lyon in 1305 and because the French College of Cardinals was extremely influential, it was decided that the Pope would simply remain in France. That was fine with the king, because it meant a boost to his influence in Europe."

"Philip the *Fair*?" Max asked, and he winked at Hellen. "Was there also a King Maximilian the Fair?"

Hellen rolled her eyes and looked to Sister Lucrezia for support.

"Let's go in, Hellen," the nun said. She hooked her arm under Hellen's, and they strode off together toward the entrance. The men marched after them, and a withering glance from Edward kept Max quiet.

"Papa, what exactly do you have in mind? Where are we supposed to start looking? Or maybe a better question: what exactly are we looking for?"

"Exactly what it looks like I can't really say. But basically, we're searching for a document that confirms King Arthur's existence."

Max gaped, looking so foolish that Hellen almost felt sorry for him.

"King Arthur is just a legend, though, isn't he?" Hellen asked, turning to her father. "Even today there's no unequivocal evidence that he ever really existed."

Edward smiled. "I was very happy to hear that Count Palffy's records were now with Blue Shield. He started the file on Arthur when we both began working here," he said earnestly.

"I can still remember when I first held his 'special' file in my hands," Hellen said, smiling. "At first I thought he was making some kind of joke at my expense. It was filled with things that serious historians and archaeologists roll their eyes at: Noah's Ark, the Golden Fleece, Atlantis, the lost Confederate gold, all sorts of things."

Edward nodded. He knew the file well.

"It was a very long time before I began to take any of it seriously," Hellen went on. "I couldn't make head or tail of most of what he had in there. After Nikolaus died, I analyzed the various documents more closely, but I still couldn't make much sense of anything."

Edward's face clouded when Hellen mentioned the death of his old friend. "I thought I knew Nikolaus. I still can't believe he was part of a terrorist organization that tried to assassinate the Pope . . . "

"And let's not forget the nuclear bomb," Hellen added.

"He always was ambitious, but I never thought he'd go that far. He and I talked a lot about King Arthur back in the day, so I knew what to look for in his records. That's what has led us here."

Sister Lucrezia had been reading through her guide book the entire time and was starting to get impatient. "Can we please go in? I'm already in a state." The nun's enthusiasm even seemed to infect Max, who normally had no interest in culture at all. "We've got so much to get through. The papal palace covers 15,000 square meters and has a very complicated layout, typical of the Middle Ages. It's very intricate, practically a labyrinth," she lectured.

"Sorry to disappoint you, Sister, but there isn't very much to see where we want to go."

Lucrezia looked at Edward in bewilderment. Hellen tried to explain.

"We're not here as tourists. We're looking for the Templar casket."

"The Templar casket?" Sister Lucrezia repeated.

"The Templars are partly to blame for the whole thing," Edward said. "The Order's wealth was always a point of contention between the Vatican and the secular rulers. Philip the Fair was the Order's biggest debtor. Basically, he hassled Pope Clemens V to dissolve the Knights Templar, then took their wealth for himself. That's the story that's been passed down, at least."

"But I thought you were here about King Arthur?" the nun said.

"That's right," Hellen agreed, turning back to her father.

Edward beamed at her. "It's nice to know I can still surprise my daughter. The history of the Templars tells us that the order was founded in Jerusalem between 1118 and 1121. But that isn't strictly true."

"Don't keep us in suspense, Papa," Hellen said, more than a little reproachfully.

"The Order of the Knights Templar was *not* founded then. Its members only needed a new name."

"So what were they called before?" Now even Max's curiosity was aroused.

"Before that, they were known as the Knights of the Round Table."

9

THE BELVEDERE, VIENNA. EAST WING

CLOUTARD VIVIDLY REMEMBERED THE LAST TIME HE HAD been in this part of Vienna: Hellen and he had watched as a bomb destroyed Tom's grandfather's apartment. Fortunately, Arthur Prey had been in Cuba at the time. Cloutard had to smile as he recalled the skirmish with the old soldier at the cigar factory in Havana.

Now, that all seemed part of another life. Too much had happened since then, and it was time he started looking out for himself again. Once, he'd ruled an empire—as a smuggler, forger and thief, Cloutard had had his fingers in practically every major crime involving art or valuable artifacts. That is, until Ossana Ibori and Absolute Freedom had taken away everything he had. But now he had a chance to take it all back. His day had come at last.

He wandered through the east wing of the summer palace, a city residence built for Prince Eugene by the Austrian baroque architect Johann Lukas von Hildebrandt.

They really knew how to live back then, Cloutard thought wistfully. His own home base in Tabarka had been modeled after the interiors of Belvedere, Schönbrunn and Versailles. But that property had been taken from him along with everything else.

Cloutard stopped before the pride of the Belvedere's collection—a world-famous painting that had caused a sensation when it was first exhibited. It wasn't quite in the same league as da Vinci's "Mona Lisa," of course, but Gustav Klimt's "The Kiss" was still a phenomenal work. His "Farm Garden with Sunflowers," for example, had sold at auction in London for 57 million euros, and his "Portrait of Adele Bloch-Bauer II" had brought 150 million dollars. It was impossible to say what Klimt's best-known work, "The Kiss," might fetch at auction. Cloutard stood several paces in front of the artwork and studied the almost six-foot-square, oil-on-canvas master-piece, the crowning work of Klimt's famous golden phase. Klimt had studied Byzantine art in Ravenna on a trip through Italy, and it had become his greatest inspiration.

"An impressive piece, isn't it?"

Cloutard glanced over his shoulder and saw a small man with a moustache and an olive complexion. He wore a hat and a rumpled suit and somehow reminded Cloutard of Columbo, probably why he hadn't noticed him at first. He was the personification of average.

"*Absolument*," Cloutard murmured and looked search-ingly at the man.

"My name is not important, but I think my accent will tell you who my clients are, at least."

Indeed. A few words had been enough for Cloutard to know who this man was. He had spent many years listening to Italian mafiosi speak, and he could recognize a *soldato* or *capo* immediately—not least because his own foster father, Don Innocenzo, had been the head of a family for years.

"What we ask of you, Francesco, is simple."

Cloutard was used to Italians speaking his first name in the Italian way. His mother did the same.

"We want you to make a copy." The man motioned vaguely in the direction of "The Kiss."

Cloutard whistled softly through his teeth. "But to what end? The whole world knows that the original is hanging here in the Belvedere. You would never be able to sell the forgery on the black market. This isn't like the 'Mona Lisa,' where no one knows for certain if the painting in the Louvre is really the original."

The Italian frowned slightly. "Let us worry about that."

Cloutard looked around. The other visitors were too far away to hear their conversation. But he held a hand over his mouth, just in case. Art thieves and forgers had been caught in the past because lip-readers had deciphered their intentions through security cameras.

"A forgery will not be easy. The gold leaf and the patina are difficult to copy. The labor and expense for such a piece would be enormous. It is not a one-man job. We would need several experts working together and a size-able budget to cover the up-front costs."

The Italian coughed loudly. The sound echoed through the east wing and several faces turned in their direction.

"Let us discuss the rest outside."

The two men left the building in silence and walked into the expansive garden at the rear of the palace. The view was breathtaking. St. Stephen's Cathedral rose above the horizon, and on clear days like today, it was possible to see as far as Vienna's vineyards and the northern border of the imperial city.

"When you deliver a perfect copy of the painting to us, the family will help you restore your interests in your old business." He paused and stroked a hand over one of the sphinxes lining the path. "We believe we can arrange things so that everything will be as it was, before that unfortunate affair with AF and the woman, Ossana, and all the unhappy consequences."

Cloutard inhaled audibly and his eyes narrowed. The offer was extremely attractive. He had no doubt whatsoever that the family would be able to deliver on their promise. He would once again be sharing tables with the truly great. He'd be back in business—the business he loved so much, and to which he had dedicated most of his life. He smiled. At first glance, of course, this would put him at odds with Blue Shield, but perhaps it would be possible to exploit the synergies involved, without having to give up either. The strategist in him was already weighing options. He was leaning toward accepting the offer.

"However, you would have to fund the project yourself," the man said, almost casually, and Cloutard's ambitious plans came crashing down like a house of cards.

"But . . . " Cloutard left the protest unspoken. There was no point, and he knew it. He could either accept the family's terms or turn down the job—but how could he even think of turning it down? He would have to rekindle some old contacts and set up interim financing.

The man looked at him enquiringly, but he knew Cloutard had nothing else to say.

"I'll be in touch again soon. Get started. The don is impatient, as I'm sure you know."

Without another word, the man turned off the path and walked toward the Prinz-Eugen-Strasse exit. Cloutard, his mind hard at work, watched the mafioso until he had left the garden. Then he took out his phone and keyed through his contact list. He was still owed a favor by Farid Shaham, whose father had been his right-hand man for years. Now was the time to call it in.

10

INSIDE THE PALAIS DES PAPES, AVIGNON, FRANCE

"ARE YOU TRYING TO TELL US THAT THE KNIGHTS TEMPLAR are basically a rebranded Knights of the Round Table?" Hellen asked.

Her father nodded.

"Okay, I'm going to have to let that digest."

Hellen had gotten used to throwing conventional history out the window. The Library of Alexandria and El Dorado had seriously readjusted her view of generally accepted historical facts—but the Knights of the Round Table was another dimension altogether.

"If you keep that in mind while you look at the façade, then the Palais could definitely have been the headquarters of the Knights Templar. It certainly looks more like a knight's castle than a papal palace," Sister Lucrezia said with audible respect in her voice.

They entered the palace through the Porte Notre Dame and immediately found themselves in the impressive inner courtyard.

"I can hardly wait to see the Pope's private rooms. The frescoes by Matteo Giovannetti are supposed to be amazing." Hellen was already grinning. Sister Lucrezia was as wide-eyed as a little girl on Christmas morning.

"It's no coincidence that the treasures of the Templars and the artifacts associated with King Arthur show similarities," Edward said with conviction.

Hellen nodded, lost in her own thoughts. "The Holy Grail," she whispered reverently.

"We're looking for the Holy Grail!?" Sister Lucrezia exclaimed—a little too loudly; they were standing among a group of visitors waiting for the guided tour to start.

"I wouldn't put it quite like that," Edward said. "We're following up some clues that Count Palffy and I discovered some years ago and in which the Templars and the Knights of the Round Table both play a role. Parts of the Templars' treasure were stored away here for some time, but good King Philip presumably squandered most of it."

"Then what exactly *are* we looking for?" Hellen asked again. Her father had still not answered that fundamental question.

"Palffy stumbled across an old myth that claimed that written records of the Round Table were supposed to exist."

"Like the minutes of a meeting?" Max asked, but Hellen and Edward ignored him.

"There are countless myths surrounding the Templars and at least as many about King Arthur. It could be a dead end, of course. But we'll know soon enough, because Palffy's clues tell us precisely where we're supposed to look."

Hellen smiled. "And I'm guessing the official tour doesn't go there, right?"

"Of course not. Many of the rooms here are not open to the public."

"Well, we're going to need permission for that. We can't just go around conducting illegal searches! Have we gone through official channels? Do we have approval?" Max asked. He had straightened up as if standing at attention and wore his best look of offense.

Hellen shook her head sadly. How was it possible that two men who'd been through the same Cobra training had come out so fundamentally different? As much as she hated to think about it just then, she was reminded even more of just how much she missed Tom. She opened her mouth to say something to Max, but her voice failed.

"No, Max, we don't!" Edward said, seeing Hellen struggling. "We're going to have to improvise a little. Somehow, we have to get from the large Jesus Hall through the Consistory Hall and into the sacristy. From there, we need to get into the chamberlain's rooms, which are situated directly below the pope's chambers. There are vaults built into the floor there, and a long stairway leads down to the basement and the Grand Treasury, and connecting passages lead off to more vaults that were operated by the financial administration, which itself is located up on the second floor of the Papal Tower. Somewhere inside this labyrinth of rooms and passages, we're supposed to find the 'Templar casket,' which supposedly contains the documents Palffy mentioned."

As Hellen, Sister Lucrezia, Edward and Max were hustled from room to room with the rest of the tour group, Sister Lucrezia's growing enthusiasm was matched only by the deep boredom etched on Max's face.

The tour took them through audience halls and rooms of extraordinary dimensions, once used for ceremonies of church and state—rooms like the large Clémentine Chapel, the pope's private rooms, including his bedchamber, and the Deer Room, with its uniquely profane pastoral frescoes.

On the way to the Saint-Martial and Saint-Jean chapels, Edward took his daughter by the arm and drew her aside. He pointed to a door blocked by nothing more than a typical museum cord.

"If this is like most of the world's museums, that cord's the only obstacle. The door behind it probably isn't even locked," Hellen whispered.

Her father grinned. "No one wants to carry around a ton of keys all the time. What do you say we let Sister Lucrezia and Max finish the tour while we go on a father-daughter treasure hunt?"

Hellen's heart swelled at the thought. She'd been dreaming about this for years, but as long as she'd believed her father was dead, she had convinced herself it was a foolish dream. The moment would be perfect if it weren't for the shadow of Tom's death.

Edward looked around for a moment, then stepped over the cord and tried the handle.

"Bingo!" Hellen said as the door swung open.

As they slipped into the corridor on the other side, the world around them changed instantly. The rooms were bare, shabby and looked in need of renovation. The fabulous rooms of state they'd been standing in a moment before made the contrast daunting.

"There's a stairway that connects all of the vaults and treasuries. Palffy and I were going through the chronicles of a man who wrote in the time directly after the dissolution of the Templars and we found a clue to a so-called 'Templar casket.' Apparently, it's set into the stairway wall. The chronicler's description wasn't particularly detailed, unfortunately, but it has to be in that connecting stairway."

Hellen looked down to see a long spiral staircase below. "We're in the right place, Papa! If I've calculated correctly, this must go down directly beside the vaults." She had her iPad in her hands and was looking at the map they'd downloaded on the plane while researching the palace.

Edward glanced at the map and nodded.

"We have to look for a *croix pattée*, like the German Iron Cross from World War I. The Templar casket is supposed to be marked with it."

The bottom of the staircase lay in complete darkness, with no windows or other portals where light could enter. Hellen took her Maglite flashlight out of her backpack. Edward was similarly equipped. Years before, when Hellen was still a young girl, her father had taught her that an archaeologist should always carry two things with them: a flashlight and a knife.

Step by step, they descended the stone stairs together. Hellen played her flashlight back and forth between the stairway under their feet and the walls around them, searching for any sign of a Templar cross while making sure not to stumble on the worn steps. The stairs went down in a tight spiral, and she and Edward stayed close together as they descended. Hellen loved being this close to her father; she had missed him so much, for so long. There they were, feeling their way down a steep, narrow stone staircase, but she felt safe and secure in his presence. Until recently, she had only felt that safe with Tom.

"Here!" her father suddenly called. Hellen turned around. Afraid of stumbling, she'd overlooked it—pale, stamped into the stone, she saw the distinctive cross.

"Let me have your knife. You do have one, don't you?" Edward said with a smile. She handed over her ever-present penknife, and he began to scratch away the mortar around the stone. Hellen's heart was pounding. She was back in her element, on the hunt for another valuable historical artifact. And she would be present when history once again had to be rewritten—and this time she would be finally able to share the moment with her father. "The mortar here is very crumbly," Edward said, and Hellen could see how the stone was now sitting only loosely in the wall. Her father slowly eased it out, and moments later, they were holding it in their hands.

The stone was hollow, and it did slightly resemble a casket. In the light of their flashlights, they saw that it contained a leather-wrapped scroll.

"Palffy was right," Edward said excitedly as he opened the leather wrapper. They both gazed at the ancient parchment it contained. It was covered with a jumble of strange symbols and half-finished lines and paragraphs —but it appeared to be incomplete.

"We'll have to take a closer look at this," Edward said, rolling the scroll back into its leather cover. They hurried back to rejoin the official tour.

A museum guard spotted them as they closed the door behind them and climbed back over the cord. He said nothing, but snapped a photo of the pair. The young woman looked vaguely familiar to him.

11

IN FRONT OF THE PALAIS DES PAPES, AVIGNON, FRANCE

SISTER LUCREZIA, GRINNING HAPPILY, EXITED THE PALACE and waved excitedly to Hellen and Edward, who were waiting by their rental car in the parking lot.

"Ah, there you are! We lost you in there. I was so enthralled by how lovely everything was that I didn't even notice you were gone. Isn't that right, Max?"

Sister Lucrezia jabbed Max in the ribs, and he nodded wearily. He had probably never been forced to suffer through so much culture at once in his life, and his soldier's brain was struggling to digest it all.

"I was particularly impressed by—" Lucrezia suddenly fell silent when she noticed the leather roll in Hellen's hand. "Did you find something?" she said, craning her neck in curiosity.

"I am officially protesting," Max said. He had planted himself in front of Hellen and her father and glared down at them reproachfully from his six-and-a-half-foot vantage point. "My orders are to ensure your safety. That's why Theresia de Mey hired me. I can't condone any of you sneaking off and not letting me do my job. This is going in my report."

Hellen rolled her eyes. *Of course an idiot like him would file a report*, she thought. "We're still in one piece, Max. All we did was go down some stairs, press a button, and hit the jackpot," she joked. "It's all good. Relax."

She paused. Hadn't she always reprimanded Tom whenever he did something reckless? She squinted, trying to hide the tears that crept into her eyes. She missed her daredevil so much, and it was in situations like this that she felt it most.

Her emotional turmoil was not lost on Sister Lucrezia, of course. She took Hellen's hand in hers, and Hellen smiled at her gratefully as she quickly wiped away her tears. "Let's go and find something to eat, and we can take a look at what you've found," the Mother Superior said. "Your Monsieur Cloutard gave me a tip: the Crèperie du Cloître. It's just a few minutes' walk from here. He says they serve the best crêpes in the south of France." And she marched off with Hellen, who was just slipping the leather roll into her backpack.

"I could eat," said Max with a shrug. His indignation at the way Hellen and her father had ignored his protective role was gone—his stomach suddenly mattered more.

As the group circled around the Palais des Papes and followed Rue de la Peyrolerie, a man on a black motorcycle watched them closely. He started the engine and raced through the narrow streets to Place des Châtaignes. He drove past them at high speed, throttling back momentarily beside Hellen and snatching the pack that she carried—as she always did—slung loosely over her right shoulder. Hellen had no time to react. She felt no more than a passing gust of air and a second later the motorcyclist had turned into Rue Carnot, her backpack in his hand.

"Great bodyguarding," she snapped at Max. He'd watched the whole scene with his mouth agape. "Tom would already be on the guy's tail," she said accusingly, pointing in the direction the rider had disappeared.

Max looked helplessly at her but made no move to do anything.

"Are you all right?" Edward asked, giving Hellen a quick hug.

"I'm fine, yes. Or actually, no. Our discovery was in there. Now it's been stolen before we even had a chance to study it. We're back where we started."

Edward frowned thoughtfully. Then he pulled away from her and took out his mobile phone. "I know an Arthurian expert. I can show him this, at least." He held out his phone to Hellen and smiled. On the display she saw a photo of the scroll.

"You took a picture? You're the best, Papa!"

Hellen kissed him on the cheek and turned back in the direction of their rental car. The others followed. "Where does your Arthurian expert live?" she asked as they went.

"We have to pay a visit to the carnival," Edward said.

"*Kölle Alaaf!*" Max called. "I was stationed in Germany for a while. The carnival in Cologne is a blast!"

"We're aiming a little higher, my boy," Edward said. "We're going to the Carnival of Venice."

12

BY THE RHÔNE RIVER, AVIGNON, FRANCE

THE MOTORCYCLIST HAD TAKEN A CIRCUITOUS ROUTE through the old, historical part of town, making sure no one was tailing him. Avignon's ancient heart, surrounded by the old city wall, lay directly beside the Rhône. He headed northeast, skirting the Université d'Avignon and passing the city gate before turning toward the river. Along the Avenue de la Synagogue he finally stopped the motorcycle under the cover of some trees.

Tom Wagner took off his helmet and set it on the tank in front of him. For a moment, he stared at his trembling hand. It had been a long time since he had seen Hellen, and suddenly all the emotions that he had successfully managed to push aside for the last six months had come flooding back.

In Hellen's world, he was no longer alive. He could not begin to imagine what she'd gone through when she had heard about his death. They had only just found their way back to each other, and then fate had thrown a wrench in the works.

Tom closed his eyes and focused. He could not let his emotions affect him. Not yet. He had a job to do. A hard job. *Would his friends ever be able to forgive him? Would they ever trust him again? Most of all, would she?*

He shook it all off, opened the backpack, and took out the leather roll. He took a picture of it, still closed, with his iPhone and sent it to Ossana. Then he replaced the document in the backpack and swung it onto his back.

His phone buzzed. He clicked the Bluetooth earbuds on and took the call.

"Congratulations," he heard Ossana's chilly voice say. "How's your girlfriend? Did you have a nice reunion?" Tom said nothing. He felt the same uncontrollable rage rising inside him again. The abject helplessness he was feeling pushed his hatred of this woman to a new level.

"What's next?" he said, ignoring her taunts.

"Meet me tomorrow at midday at the Gran Caffè Quadri on Piazza San Marco in Venice. I'll explain the rest then."

Without a word, Tom hung up. He put the phone away inside his jacket, pulled on the helmet and, tires squealing, sped away.

13

SELLIN PIER, BY THE BALTIC SEA, ISLAND OF RÜGEN, GERMANY

"Your tea, Mr. Brice. Earl Grey with milk, steeped for precisely two hundred seconds, as usual."

The waiter set the tray down in front of the gray-haired man, Berlin Brice, known to most of the people he did business with as the Welshman. The man sitting opposite had also heard the nickname many times.

"Don't beat around the bush, Jansen," the Welshman said tersely. "The Baltic in winter is lovely, but it's not enough. I hope for your sake that I've come all this way for a good reason."

He looked impatiently at the man, then scanned the pub around him. The view beyond the windows was breathtaking. The spa town of Sellin was perched a hundred feet or so above the ocean on the eastern coast of Rügen, Germany's largest island. The pier, more than four hundred yards long, was the town's most famous landmark. After World War II the pier had been rebuilt according to historical pictures from 1927, in the classic resort style typical of Germany's Baltic coast. It lent the town a rather fashionable atmosphere. Sightseeing boats often tied up at the end of the pier, which was also how the Welshman had arrived.

Peter Jansen wiped the sweat from his forehead with his napkin. He had heard a lot of stories about the Welshman, many of which did not paint a very appealing picture of the man at all. But he had no other choice. His sources had told him unanimously that Brice was the right man—in fact, the only man—for the project he had in mind. His voice trembled as he leaned toward the Welshman.

"Klaus Störtebeker's treasure," he whispered, looking around warily to make sure no one was eavesdropping. But it was the off-season and the pub was practically empty.

"God, not this pirate story again. You'd better have more to offer me than all the other treasure hunters who've pissed me off in the past."

Jansen nodded eagerly. "But of course, Mr. Brice. We have found some very concrete clues. The documents we have are based on a number of completely independent sources. We have never been as close as we are now. Unfortunately, we need a certain amount of infrastructure, manpower, and financial backing to raise the treasure."

"Which is where I come in, I suppose." Brice set down his teacup and nodded favorably. "You know, you northern Germans really do brew a decent cup of tea. Okay, Jansen"—the Welshman flipped open his gold pocket watch—"you've got fifteen minutes to convince me. Starting now."

This was Jansen's cue. But just as he launched into the presentation he'd probably practiced dozens of times, the Welshman's phone rang. The ringtone was "*Hen Wlad Fy Nhadau*," the Welsh national anthem. Jansen had been in Wales many times and recognized the haunting music immediately. He paused, exhaled, and pointed disapprovingly at the phone.

The Welshman took the call.

"Mr. Brice? It's Léon Duvasseur from Avignon. Sir, it seems someone has found the Templar casket."

The Welshman jumped to his feet, rattling the glasses and cups on the table in front of him. Jansen had to catch the vase of flowers, which would otherwise have toppled over.

The Welshman's phone pinged: a message.

"I've just sent you a photo of the people I thought looked suspicious," Duvasseur said. "And I've searched the area they were sniffing around. I found a hollow brick marked with the Templar cross, but it was empty."

The Welshman was hyperventilating. He sat down again and looked at the picture.

"Thanks, Duvasseur. You've earned a bonus."

The Welshman ended the call and snapped his fingers. One of his two bodyguards, sitting at the next table, jumped to his feet and leaned down to his boss.

"Activate the network. Everybody. Everyone who's ever worked for us. Inform them all. No exceptions."

He held the phone with the picture under the bodyguard's nose. "Send them this photo. These two have whatever was inside the Templar casket. There's a million in cash for whoever brings it to me, and a hundred grand for anyone who tells me where they're staying. The woman is Hellen de Mey, historian and special agent of Blue Shield."

The Welshman was back on his feet again. He looked down at Peter Jansen apologetically. "No disrespect, Mr. Jansen, but I have a far more important project to attend to. In six hundred years, no one has discovered Störtebeker's treasure. A few more days won't make much difference."

Flanked by his bodyguards, the Welshman hurried out of the pub and strode down the pier.

"I'll be putting this bill on my next expense account. You can count on that," Jansen muttered to himself, putting twenty euros on the table and leaving the pub as well.

14

GRAN CAFFÈ QUADRI, PIAZZA SAN MARCO, VENICE, ITALY

THE SMALL WATER TAXI STOPPED AT THE PONTE DELLA Paglia, a tiny historic footbridge, and Tom climbed up the few steps from the dock. He followed Riva degli Schiavoni and turned right onto Piazza San Marco. On his left loomed one of the symbols of the northern Italian city: the monolithic clock tower known as the Campanile, standing more than three hundred feet high. Off to the right was the impressive Basilica of St. Mark. Construction on the building, with its five distinctive domes, had started in 1063 and continued over more than three centuries. Renovations had been carried out in the early 17th century, bringing the cathedral to its current splendor. On the square in front of the church, three ships' masts had towered since 1480, flying pennants on Sundays and public holidays.

Tom crossed the historic square, scattering pigeons. The square, known partially for the vast numbers of pigeons it attracted, was crowded today with both tourists and artisans of every description. Preparations for Carnival—

it started the following day—were in full swing. Police barriers were in place, workers were erecting a gigantic video wall, and the steel cables for the Flight of the Angel were being raised into position. The traditional spectacle would open the Venice Carnival, as it did every year: starting from the Campanile, a young woman would swoop across the Piazza San Marco. The younger generation would be more likely to recognize Venice from the hit video game "Assassin's Creed," from images of the character Desmond Miles leaping acrobatically across the rooftops of the city.

The arcades of the Procuratie buildings that framed the square on three sides housed countless small businesses and venerable, overpriced coffee shops. Tom crossed to the north side of the square and headed directly for the Gran Caffè Quadri. He spotted Ossana from a distance, sitting at a small table under the roofed section of the café—the African woman was as beautiful as she was dangerous. He sat down at her table without a word. A waiter was with them instantly, asking for their orders.

"*Un caffè per favore*," said Tom. Ossana just shook her head when the waiter turned to her.

"*Mi piacerebbe molto*," the waiter said, and disappeared again.

"Did you bring me something pretty?" Ossana asked. Tom looked at her and smiled.

"So you really think I'd be stupid enough to carry it with me? The scroll's in a safe place, don't worry. You'll get everything as soon as I have the antidote for Hellen's father in my hands."

Ossana, leaning back in her chair with her long legs crossed in front of her, now sat forward and moved uncomfortably close to Tom. Her gloved hand clawed into Tom's thigh under the table. "Have it your way," she hissed, and slid a satellite phone across the table. "You can reach me on that anytime, anywhere. And vice versa."

Tom took the phone. Noah had presumably already been at it. After his accident, he'd transformed himself from one of Mossad's best field agents into a talented hacker. And he'd used his skills to save Tom's ass more than once.

Ossana let go of Tom's leg when the waiter returned with his espresso.

"*Grazie*," said Ossana, with a fake smile.

Tom nodded, leaned back, and sipped at the hot coffee. "What now?" he asked.

Ossana took a small note from a pocket of her trench coat and pushed it across to him.

"Your next destination," she said. Tom took the note and glanced at it. An address. "The unofficial opening ball for Carnival takes place there tonight. It's a masked ball, and everyone who's anyone in Venice will be there."

"How am I supposed to get inside?"

"That's for you to figure out. You're a clever boy. You'll think of something."

"And what do I do there?" Tom was getting a little peeved.

"You're looking for Lord Ernest Whitlock. He's an expert on everything to do with King Arthur, and he's also the man hosting on the ball. He has a weakness for medieval stuff, so he shouldn't be two hard to spot among all the baroque costumes. He'll be able to help you find the next piece. A little gentle persuasion should do the trick."

Wonderful. Now I'm supposed to torture an old man to extract information, Tom thought. *What's next?*

Ossana stood up and left a few euros on the table.

"Remember what's at stake. Do what I tell you, and your girlfriend's father will have a long, happy life ahead of him." She turned away and left Tom sitting at the table. "Have fun at the ball!" she called back without turning around.

Tom finished his espresso and left the café as well.

15

"I HAVE COME TO ASK YOU FOR THAT FAVOR." THE SOUND of Cloutard's voice sent Farid Shaham into a violent coughing fit, but he just managed to avoid spitting his shrimp curry across the table. Cloutard patted him on the back. "Come, Farid. Charlie's is famous for its curry. It would be such a waste."

Cloutard, grinning broadly, had taken the seat next to Farid. Opposite them sat two men, now looking the Frenchman up and down in surprise. Farid had almost recovered. Glassy-eyed and still coughing, he turned to the two men. "You will have to excuse me. We can continue our talk soon, but I'm going to need a few minutes."

Nettled, the two men stood up and moved silently inside to the bar of the trendy Heliopolis restaurant.

Cloutard and Farid had not met since the whole Library of Alexandria affair. For many years, Farid's father Karim had been Cloutard's right hand in his smuggling organization. When Karim was murdered, Farid had held Cloutard responsible. And because Farid needed money, he had tried to extort it from Cloutard. Fortunately for both, they had come to a mutually satisfactory arrangement—in fact, Farid had ended up owing Cloutard a little help.

"What do you want, François?"

Farid's tone was reserved. He remembered the day in Tuscany very well indeed—and the goodwill that both Cloutard and his mother had shown toward him. And he also owed Cloutard for the part he had played in saving his daughter's life. Whatever Cloutard wanted in return, it was bound to be substantial.

"I am letting you off lightly, my friend. I just need some of your father's records. Specifically, the folder where he listed all of our contacts. You know the one."

Farid smiled mischievously. "You would really have been lost without my father, wouldn't you?"

Cloutard nodded sheepishly, but quickly recovered. His French ego could not let a remark like that go unchallenged.

"*Excuse-moi.* I was running an international enterprise. One cannot do everything oneself." Cloutard waved the waiter over. "I sincerely hope they have—"

Farid cut him off: "Yes, they do."

Farid was well aware of the Frenchman's preferences, and he ordered two glasses of Louis XIII, the most expensive bottled cognac in the world. The waiter raised his eyebrows in surprise but nodded.

"You weren't running an 'international enterprise,' François. You were running a major criminal gang," Farid said with a malicious smile.

Cloutard ignored the slight and sipped contentedly from his brandy snifter.

"Tomato, tomahto," he said and gesticulated in Farid's direction as if shooing away an annoying fly. "Where are your father's papers?"

"At our house. It's not far from here. I can bring them to you tomorrow. Which hotel are you staying at? St. Regis, as usual?"

Cloutard grimaced. "I can't wait that long. I need them now."

Farid tilted his head slightly. He knew Cloutard, and this wasn't like him. He was nervous, even agitated. It was obviously important to him to get his hands on the documents. Farid nodded earnestly. "No problem, François. We can go and get them right now. We'll just have to keep our voices down."

Cloutard finished the last of his cognac in a single swallow. Farid's eyes widened. Cloutard was really in a hurry. Louis XIII was practically worshipped, certainly not something to knock back like cheap booze.

"We will not disturb Armeen or your daughter Shamira, I promise."

Cloutard was on his feet, had laid a few bills on the table, and was preparing to leave. Farid gave the two men he'd been talking to earlier an apologetic call-you-later signal. Cloutard was already out in the street, flagging a taxi.

Minutes later, they climbed out at Farid's house. Palms surrounded the front garden, the lawn was as green as an English golf course, and the flower beds and gravel paths were testament to a degree of wealth rarely found in the Egyptian capital.

Cloutard whistled through his teeth.

"I am impressed, Farid. You have done well for yourself."

"I've got a new business partner. Armeen connected us."

The crossed a central courtyard where a fountain babbled cheerfully. Some of the objets d'art decorating the courtyard seemed somehow familiar to Cloutard. Farid fished out a bunch of keys and opened a large gate that led from the courtyard directly into his office. It was clear to see that Farid had hit the jackpot with whatever business he was now in. He was almost bursting with curiosity. Who was Farid's new partner? Was his obviously flourishing business really above board? Farid pulled a chair up to a large tapestry and climbed onto it. He pushed the tapestry aside to reveal a modern safe built into the wall. *Not exactly an antique*, Cloutard thought, as he watched a retinal scanner read Farid's right eye. A moment later, the safe hissed and opened. It very large, and it took a while before Farid managed to dig back to the folder that Cloutard wanted. Together, they went to the desk and Farid opened the leather document case. Cloutard froze. He turned and looked accusingly at Farid.

"I'm sorry, François. I had no idea, please believe me,"

Farid stammered. His eyes switched back and forth between Cloutard's angry face and the empty case in front of them.

"Tell it to someone more gullible than me. Are you seriously trying to tell me that someone stole the papers from your safe?" Cloutard crossed to the open door of the vault. "Your high-tech safe with its retinal scanner?"

Cloutard's voice had grown loud, and he slammed the heavy steel door shut.

"I don't check it every day. I don't know how long they've been missing. I . . . I have no idea how this could even happen."

"*Naturellement!* You have a state-of-the-art safe, but somehow you are not very sure what you have inside it?" Cloutard sighed audibly. "Farid, is this gratitude?" He brought his hand down hard onto the desk and the sound rang through the courtyard. "I helped save your daughter's life, and now you try to weasel out with some flimsy excuse?"

Cloutard had returned to Farid as he spoke, and now only a few inches separated their faces. Cloutard's glare was practically burning Farid's skin.

"What's going on here?"

The two men spun to see Armeen, Farid's wife, in a billowing white nightdress, standing barefoot in the doorway of the office. They exchanged a glance.

"Nothing, my darling. Everything's okay," Farid said calmly, and he went to his wife. "François needs a few documents that we can't seem to find just now."

Cloutard's annoyance had dissipated a little, and his old Gallic charm returned as he crossed to Armeen and kissed her hand. "I apologize for being so loud, but it is a matter of utmost importance," he said.

A little embarrassed, Armeen drew Cloutard, her daughter's savior, close and embraced him warmly.

"Ah, *those* papers," Armeen said as she looked over Cloutard's shoulder. She released him and went to the desk, where the leather folder lay empty. Farid and Cloutard looked on in confusion.

"Mr. Brice picked them up a few weeks ago."

Cloutard's mouth hung open for several long seconds. Then he slumped into an armchair in disbelief and turned to Farid.

"Please don't tell me the Welshman is your new business partner."

16

HOTEL DANIELI, VENICE, ITALY

"WHY EXACTLY DO WE HAVE TO GO TO THE BALL IN THESE stupid costumes?" Max was just buttoning the vest beneath his rococo tailcoat and kept tugging at the white plastron wrapped around his neck. "And you can bet your life I'm never going to wear this hat again. I'm a soldier in one of the top anti-terror units in the world, not a damn clown." He picked up the crimson tricorn hat with the gold trim and threw it carelessly onto the couch.

Edward came into the living room from his bedroom and smiled mildly. He stopped in front of the mirror and adjusted his own outfit a little. "As I said on the drive, Lord Ernest Whitlock is an eccentric of the first order, the classic mad scientist. He lives a completely secluded life and you have no chance of getting close to him. He's extremely rich and he lives in a hotel—need I say more? He has the entire top floor to himself and he's protected by countless bodyguards. He only leaves his penthouse once a year to mingle in the hustle and bustle of society. And that's today, at his annual costume ball."

"So I have to show up dressed like some mincing Mozart in knickerbockers, knee-length socks and a silly mask?"

"Sorry, Max, but you don't have a choice," Hellen said, also entering the living room. She wore a wide, flouncing Marie Antoinette-style dress that complemented her father's outfit. The floor-length, burgundy ensemble consisted of a wide hooped skirt with a corset waist, decorated with elaborate gold lace. Hellen was struggling to breathe in it and was worried that it pushed her breasts up too far. "If anyone has a right to complain, it's me. Look what I have to deal with! If I ever have to go to the bathroom, I'll be out of circulation for an hour." She puffed and panted as she lifted the dress to reveal the countless petticoats underneath. "And if I do, one of you is going to have to help me!" she added with a grin, enjoying the shocked looks on the men's faces. "I can hardly breathe and I'm already dying of heat exhaustion in this." She fluttered her fan dramatically as she went on: "And Max, weren't you complaining in Avignon about how we went off on our own? So do your job, watch our backs, and stop grumbling."

She did not sound cheerful at all. Edward and Max both raised their eyebrows, and Max had also raised his hands in appeasement: he'd do what she asked. "All right, all right. Take it easy," he said.

Hellen was standing in front of the wall mirror now and turned a full circle.

"These things are damned uncomfortable, and I have no idea how women were ever able to wear them," she said. "But it's very, very lovely."

"It is. You look like a princess," her father said proudly, and Max rolled his eyes with irritation. Hellen beamed.

She played around with her pinned-up hair a little and practiced a courtly curtsey for her father.

"Pa-paaaaaaaa," she said with a French accent, drawing out the second "a" for several seconds, "we can go now."

"It's very practical, working for UNESCO, isn't it? There are always last-minute tickets to be had." The concierge had brought them up earlier, and Edward now put the tickets away in his pocket.

"And last-minute costumes," Hellen added. "Even for our baroque sourpuss here." She waved her fan at Max as he grimly picked up his tricorn hat to leave.

"Everyone got their masks? No mask, no entry," Edward said firmly.

Hellen rolled her eyes. "You can't go anywhere without a mask in this town. It's like being back in that stupid pandemic."

They left the room and made their way down the elegant staircase of the palazzo, which had been built in the 14th century by the Dandolo family.

Hellen leaned close to her father. "You know we're in good company here, don't you?"

Edward nodded. "Of course. Goethe, Wagner, Dickens, and Lord Byron all stayed here. And now they can add the famous de Mey dynasty." He put his arm around his daughter and gave her an affectionate hug.

For a brief moment, Hellen remembered her last visit to

a ball with Tom: the Opera Ball in Vienna. But the sad recollection dissolved when they reached the foot of the stairs and turned the corner to find themselves at the entrance to the magnificent ballroom.

"We have to find Lord Whitlock, although I don't imagine it will be difficult," said Edward thoughtfully. "He'll probably be the only one wearing a medieval costume among all the rococo finery. We'll only have a brief moment, if that, to show him the photo of the scroll from the Templar casket."

"And then hope he'll be interested enough to grant us an audience and grace us with his expertise," Hellen added.

The three of them pushed their way into the masses of revellers. They had landed in another world. The history of Venice's legendary carnival could be traced all the way back to the 12th century, and it had seen its share of highs and lows in that time. The heyday of its pomp and decadence had been in Casanova's time, but it had languished during Napoleon's rule and the *Risorgimento*, the period of Italian reunification in the 19th century. In the 20th century, though, the carnival had once again grown to its deserved greatness.

"Did you know that a Vivienne Westwood design called 'The Mists of Avalon' once won the prize for the most beautiful costume," said Hellen, peering left and right at the exquisite masks and fancy costumes and at the same time watching for Lord Whitlock's unmistakable costume. "Maybe that's a good omen for our quest."

Edward pointed ahead to a large private box set up close to the stage. The orchestra members had not yet taken their places, but the private boxes for honored guests were already full.

"A very good omen indeed," Hellen said. "What a coincidence. A Knight Templar outfit—I believe we've found our lord."

"Indeed," said Edward. He took Hellen by the hand, and they edged forward, Max bringing up the rear. He seemed to have gotten used to his outfit and had adopted his usual military vigilance, scrutinizing everyone who came too close to Hellen and Edward, which kept him quite busy.

———

"'Have fun at the ball!' Oh, I will," Tom murmured to himself and looked up thoughtfully at the façade of the Hotel Danieli. He had to get inside somehow, but with neither ticket nor costume it wasn't going to be easy. The area around the entrance was cordoned off. He stood to one side in a dark corner and watched the comings and goings in front of the hotel, the guests in their magnificent garb streaming in from the direction of St. Mark's Square. Others disembarked from boats and gondolas. All of them, before they entered the palazzo, stopped and posed for the countless photographers gathered in front of the luxurious hotel.

He looked out over the lagoon, shimmering in the moonlight in front of the hotel. His mind was racing, and he almost overlooked the group that had just landed at the large hotel jetty. All of them were dressed in identical baroque costumes.

Definitely on their way to the ball, he thought.

He watched as one of them split from the group and trotted back to the boat, where he seemed to have left something on board. This was Tom's chance. He hurried down to the landing stage and ducked behind the hotel's boathouse. Seconds later, the man returned. Tom dragged him behind the boathouse, and a little pressure on the man's carotid artery rendered him unconscious. Tom kept a wary eye on the rest of the group. Luckily, the man's friends seemed to be in no particular hurry. They were standing at the entrance to Calle de le Rasse, a narrow laneway that belonged to the hotel, where a bar had been set up for welcome drinks—the group was standing together, drinking prosecco and gearing up for the evening ahead.

A few minutes later, Tom's transformation was complete. The costume he'd taken from the unknown man was a size too small, but it would have to do. Tom deposited the half-naked man in an empty gondola bobbing on the canal waters behind the boathouse, presumably waiting for repairs, and threw a tarpaulin over his unconscious body. Fortunately, everyone's attention was focused on the spectacle in front of the hotel, and he could do what he had to unnoticed. He set the tricorn hat on his head, pulled the mask over his face, and hurried over to join the group at the prosecco stand, hoping that his Italian would hold up long enough for him to smuggle himself into the palazzo with the others.

17

INTERPOL ŞUBE MÜDÜRLÜĞÜ (INTERPOL BRANCH OFFICE), ISTANBUL

VITTORIA ARCANO HAD NOT WORKED IN THE FIELD SINCE the assignment in Ethiopia. And although she had done an excellent job there, since then her work had been restricted to administrative duties—a nice way to describe the boredom that her job at Blue Shield HQ in Vienna involved.

Now, stepping into the Interpol bureau in Istanbul, she automatically recalled her first day at Interpol in her homeland, Italy. It had all been so exciting: she had met Tom by accident in Rome, and together they had foiled a terrorist group on board a high-speed train. She'd wanted to experience it again, that adrenaline rush of working with him in a life-or-death situation. In that frame of mind, she'd switched from Interpol to Blue Shield—which had been something of a letdown, to put it lightly. But maybe that was about to change.

She walked to the front desk and an officer looked up.

"Vittoria Arcano," she said. "I'm with UNESCO; I'm here about the two missing Blue Shield employees."

The man nodded and stood up. "You need to talk to the boss," he said, and he tilted his head, indicating that she should follow him.

Nehir Dursun, who ran the Interpol National Central Bureau in Istanbul, cut an imposing figure. For a Turkish woman, Nehir was exceptionally tall and powerfully built. Vittoria estimated that she was at least six-foot-one. She wore her hair short and had piercing eyes that immediately commanded respect. Vittoria doubted she had had an easy life as a woman in Turkey. The conservative attitudes that had been creeping back ever since the good days under Atatürk demanded a daily battle that had left its marks in the lines of her face.

"Welcome to Istanbul, Ms. Arcano," she said in flawless English. "It must be like a homecoming for you, here in our office." Nehir had clearly done her homework on Vittoria. "Unfortunately, I'm not able to tell you anything new. Your two colleagues are still officially considered missing, and the police have nothing to go on. It's as if they vanished into thin air."

Vittoria nodded thoughtfully.

"I think I'll start with their hotel rooms. Maybe I'll find something there. They were actually only here to examine a few new finds with the director of the Topkapi Palace Museum."

"From what I understand of Blue Shield, you operate in war zones and are often up against terrorists," Nehir said. "But this should have been a completely risk-free assignment. I regret very much that something has happened to your colleagues here."

"I believe they were based at the Shangri-La Hotel. Can you contact the hotel management and tell them I'm coming to look at their rooms?"

"Of course. Give me your mobile number and I'll be in touch the moment I hear anything new."

Vittoria wrote her number down for Nehir. Then she looked up and said, "By the way, I'm staying in the Ciragan Palace Kempinski and I still have to check in there. I've come straight from the airport."

"Should I have one of our people assigned to you, as escort and interpreter?"

Vittoria thought about the offer for a moment, but declined. She could not trust anyone. She knew how poorly Interpol officers were paid, and she wouldn't be at all surprised to discover that everyone around her was on someone's payroll. She'd be better off working alone.

"Thanks, but I'll manage," she said. "But I'd be very grateful if you could arrange a taxi for me."

A few minutes later, she was on her way to the Shangri-La Hotel. The concierge was waiting for her with the room keys ready and went with her to the second floor. The electronic lock blinked green and the concierge opened the door.

The man uttered a curse in his native tongue, and a moment later Vittoria saw the reason for it. The room had clearly been thoroughly ransacked.

"No one has been in here since the police came," the concierge said, his expression a mix of bewilderment and apology.

"Well, that's obviously not true," Vittoria said, moving around the room. Cupboards stood open, clothes lay strewn on the floor, drawers had been emptied. The scene in the bathroom was similarly chaotic. A minute later, they discovered that the second room was in a similar state. Vittoria glared fiercely at the concierge.

"I will ask housekeeping immediately if they noticed anything. I can only extend my humblest apologies," the man said. "I cannot explain how this could happen."

Vittoria's telephone rang. She answered.

"Miss Arcano?" It was Nehir Dursun. "I have bad news. The police have found two bodies in the Cisterna Basilica. They appear to be your colleagues."

18

THE HOTEL DANIELI BALLROOM

Tom was surprised to find that the group he had joined did not use the main entrance, but instead entered the hotel through the service entrance on Calle de le Rasse. He had a bad feeling about that. He hoped he hadn't gotten himself into a situation that would get him exposed. He followed the twenty-five or so others along several corridors until they came to a large room that functioned as a dressing room for the entire group—and as he entered, everything became clear.

Musical instruments were scattered on tables in the room: violins, violas, flutes, oboes and bassoons. Cellos leaned against the walls. Tom's pulse began to race. He'd learned several instruments from his mother in his child-hood, but the only one he could really play well was the piano. He'd spent years playing Broadway classics from the "Great American Songbook" in a bar in Vienna as a kind of counterbalance to his duties in the Cobra anti-terror unit. He could still occasionally be found in a piano bar when time permitted, but his audience usually consisted of the bar employees and cleaning staff, just before closing time.

This was a baroque orchestra, which meant his only chance was if the guy he'd put to sleep at the boathouse was the harpsichordist. If not, the jig was up.

The men and women began tuning their instruments and preparing for the performance. Tom was starting to sweat, but incredibly no instruments remained when the others started to head out to the stage. He sighed with relief. *Okay, you're a little rusty, but it's baroque music,* Tom thought. All he had to do was play the *basso continuo* with the cello. The *basso continuo* was the general bass line, consisting of the harmonies that accompanied the solo instruments. In the baroque period, the *basso continuo* usually wasn't even notated exactly, but improvised. *I ought to be able to manage that,* he thought. At the same time, he could keep watch from the stage for his target, the only man who would be dressed in medieval garb.

Tom entered the stage with the other musicians and quickly found his seat at the harpsichord. The first piece on the program was a classic: "Spring" from Vivaldi's *The Four Seasons*. Personally, he would have preferred Haydn's *Farewell Symphony*, but he didn't think anyone was about to do him that favor. The concertmaster, who led the group—as was customary for baroque orchestras, there was no conductor—stood and began the first movement. Tom played the chords mechanically, paying attention to the concertmaster's tempo, and let his eyes roam the gathered guests. Not far from the stage, he quickly caught sight of a man wearing a red cross on his chest. The costume was so different from the others that it had to be his man. He could not let him out of his sight before the orchestra took their first break, which he guessed would come after the second concerto, "Summer."

Suddenly, Tom saw a woman behind the knight, straightening her mask. Tom caught the briefest glimpse of her face, but the shock was enough to make him almost lose the tempo. He would have sworn that he had just seen Hellen.

————

"Lord Whitlock has no interest in speaking with you. He is here to enjoy himself. This is his ball and he will be spending his time only with his personal guests in his private box." The bodyguard glowered at Hellen, Edward and Max. "It's called privacy."

Hellen had briefly removed her mask to give the bodyguard her most charming smile.

"Then at least show him this photograph, please." Edward held his iPhone under the boorish man's nose. Unimpressed by either Hellen's smile or the picture, the bodyguard firmly pushed Edward's arm aside.

"I repeat, Lord Whitlock is receiving no visitors today, for any reason." The bodyguard was starting to get annoyed, now. As far as he was concerned, the matter was at an end. He squared himself at the front of the entrance to the private box and hustled the trio of visitors away.

"Please. We're from Blue Shield," Hellen begged. "It's an organization that will certainly mean something to Lord Whitlock. We've come especially—" But Hellen's pleading was drowned out by thunderous applause. On stage, "Summer" had just ended. Intermission.

Edward drew his daughter aside. As the applause gradually ebbed, the first guests began to leave their places. "Let it go," Edward said. "We'll find another way."

They moved off a short distance, but kept an eye on the private box. The corridor gradually filled with guests making their way to the bars or the bathrooms. The musicians, too, left the stage, disappearing through a door to the backstage area not far from Lord Whitlock's box.

"This is our chance!" Hellen said. She nudged her father and pointed toward the door of the box, which was just opening. A man dressed as a Knight Templar emerged. Hellen grabbed Max by the arm and pulled him down to her level. "Your job is to deal with the bodyguard. I don't care what you do, just keep him off our backs for a few seconds." She gave Max a push as Lord Whitlock and his personal guard edged through the crowd. Countless guests wanted to pay their respects and congratulate the man on his party. Like a Hollywood star mobbed by fans, the introverted nobleman pushed past them all. His bodyguard had his hands full forging a path through the milling crowd, and Max, taken off balance by Hellen's push, stumbled into him.

"Now or never," Hellen said, and she pulled her father after her and stopped right in Lord Whitlock's path. The host, his head down and eyes on the floor, had not noticed his guard's distraction and was continuing to push through the crowd.

"Lord Whitlock, we must speak with you." Hellen was holding her father's phone under his nose. "We've found the Templar casket," she added. But just at that moment, the bodyguard managed to free himself from Max's bumbling efforts and was charging back toward Hellen and her father. But he stopped in his tracks when his boss's hand suddenly shot up.

"It's all right, Ruggiero," Lord Whitlock said, his eyes fixed on the phone. "Where did you get that?" He took the phone in his hand, examining the picture closely.

"In Avignon. We—"

"That's exactly what we want to talk to you about," Edward cut in, interrupting his daughter. "Can we speak somewhere in private?"

"I definitely want to take a closer look at that," Lord Whitlock said enthusiastically. "Meet me in my pent-house after the concert. My assistant, Ruggiero Torrinelli"—he nodded toward his bodyguard—"will show you the way. Now if you'll excuse me . . ." He handed the phone back to Edward and Torrinelli bundled Hellen and her father aside. Overjoyed, they could only stand and grin at each other.

"Never do anything like that again," Max complained when he appeared beside them a moment later. His face was screwed up in pain and he was massaging his shoulder, which Torrinelli had apparently twisted painfully.

"Oh, don't be like that. You're a super-soldier, aren't you?" Hellen said, and she rolled her eyes. Max, chagrined, trotted behind her and Edward as they left the ballroom.

19

HOTEL DANIELI

IT HAD BEEN UNSPEAKABLY DIFFICULT FOR TOM NOT TO reveal himself to Hellen. No more than two feet had separated them as she exchanged a few words with Lord Whitlock. Tom wanted nothing more than to take her in his arms there and then and tell her he wasn't dead, he was alive and well, and that he . . . *pull yourself together*, he berated himself, interrupting his runaway thoughts.

He had eavesdropped on the brief conversation between Hellen and Lord Whitlock and decided that Vivaldi's "Autumn" and "Winter" would have to take place without him. He had to stick to Lord Whitlock. With a heavy heart, he let Hellen and her father move away and stayed as close as he dared to the lord.

Whitlock went only a short distance before he drew his bodyguard to one side.

"This is sensational," Whitlock said. "If those two have really found the Templar casket, I will have to get started on some research immediately."

"But, sir? What about the ball? Your guests?"

"I don't give a damn about any of that, and I know *The Four Seasons* by heart. I have more important things to deal with now. Bring them both to me immediately."

"Yes, sir," Torrinelli said with an obedient nod, and he radioed another guard to escort the lord to his suite. When the security man arrived, Torrinelli left his boss in his colleague's care and went in search of Hellen and Edward.

———

"*Andiamo. Andrà avanti presto.*" A man wearing the same costume as Tom was suddenly tugging him by his arm. Tom switched gears quickly when he saw the man's outfit. His shoulders slumped, his face contorted, and he doubled over, holding his stomach.

"*Non posso, mis sento male,*" he stammered in broken Italian. He pulled free and left the perplexed musician behind as he followed the Knight Templar through the crowd.

When they left the ballroom, the knight and his new guard approached a restricted area where another security man was stationed. Again and again, guests in bombastic costumes tried to approach the lord but all were firmly rebuffed by security. At the roped-off section, the sentry standing guard opened the barrier and let the two men pass.

You're not getting through there without drawing too much attention to yourself, Tom told himself. He could only stand and watch as the doors of a private elevator closed in front of Lord Whitlock and his bodyguard.

He recalled hearing the word "penthouse" earlier, raced out front to the lobby and found the stairs. He looked up. The venerable old stairway was an array of pillars, arches and balustrades. He sprinted up the red-carpeted stairs to the top floor and hurried down the long gallery toward the back of the building, which would lead him directly to the elevator.

When he heard the ding of the elevator arriving, Tom ducked out of sight into a window bay. He removed his mask and peered around the corner of his hiding place in time to see Lord Whitlock enter his penthouse. The security man took up position in front of the lord's door and stared stolidly straight ahead.

Tom had to get rid of the guy. He thought for a second and looked around. There was no one else in sight. The music from the ballroom drifted up to his ears—the orchestra was doing just fine without him, as he'd known they would. He donned his mask again and, staggering and mumbling, stepped out of his hiding place. He staggered toward the bodyguard, whose tension increased the closer Tom got.

"*Dove andate?*" the security guy said sternly when Tom came to a swaying stop in front of him.

"Excuse me, sir," Tom slurred in his best English, raising an index finger, "but I don't seem to be able to find the bathroom." Then he deliberately toppled toward the man, whose immediate reaction was to reach out and catch Tom under the arms—a big mistake, and exactly what Tom was counting on. In the blink of an eye, Tom had seized the man's gun from inside his jacket and was holding it under his surprised nose. Tom pressed a finger to his lips, signaled to the man to stay calm, and waved to the right with the pistol. The guard stalked ahead of Tom, and when they reached a storeroom, Tom ordered him to open the door. A hard blow to the back of his head sent him to sleep. The man fell forward neatly into the room, and all Tom had to do was lift his feet in after him.

Tom ran back to the suite, pushed the door open and stepped into the penthouse, the pistol leveled in front of him. The suite seemed to have several entrances, because Tom found himself not in an anteroom, as he had expected, but in an office filled with books and works of art. Gold silk wallpaper, baroque furniture and large oil paintings decorated the high-ceilinged office. Behind the desk sat Lord Whitlock in his Knight Templar costume, his hands in the air, looking fearfully back at Tom. The man's eyes seemed to be twitching nervously, and at the last moment Tom realized that Whitlock was trying to warn him.

He spun around just in time to fend off a blow from behind, raising his gun hand as he swung around and deflecting the dark figure's attack. The man had tried to brain him with the butt of his gun, and the blow was so powerful that it knocked the pistol from Tom's grasp. He staggered back. The attacker, in full motorcycle gear, turned his own gun on Tom, but Tom was faster: he grabbed the man's forearm and pushed up, simultaneously driving his knee into the man's gut. Locked together, they slammed against the wall, the table and cupboards, bullets flying from the attacker's gun.

They crashed into a sideboard, toppling a vase. Tom slammed the hand holding the pistol several times against the edge of the sideboard until he finally let go. A sharp punch to the man's solar plexus gave Tom the upper hand. He grabbed the slumped man by the collar and hurled him with all his strength into the middle of the room, where he crashed awkwardly into a small side table and slid to the floor. Tom bent down for the attacker's silenced pistol, but as he straightened, he realized that one of the bullets had struck Lord Whitlock.

The momentary distraction was enough for the leather-clad intruder to make his escape. He grabbed a small stool standing beside the table and hurled it at Tom, then leaped to his feet and disappeared through the open balcony door. *Probably where he got in*, Tom thought as he dodged the stool and squeezed off two futile shots after the fugitive. He tossed the empty gun aside and snatched up the security guard's pistol, tucked it into his waistband, and ran around the desk. He lifted the injured Lord Whitlock from his chair and laid him on the floor.

"Hang on," he said, pressing his hand onto the wound to try to somehow stop the bleeding, but it was too late. The man died where he lay.

At that moment, the office door opened. Tom drew his pistol with his blood-smeared hand and spun around.

Everything froze.

Tom was staring into the horrified faces of Hellen, Edward and Max.

20

A WINE CELLAR IN ČEJKOVICE, SOUTH MORAVIA, CZECH REPUBLIC

FRANÇOIS CLOUTARD CLIMBED OUT OF HIS RENTAL CAR IN front of Čejkovice Palace. The first thing that caught his eye was an old sign adorning one of the vintner's houses that bordered the palace: "*Sklep templářských rytířů.*"

Cloutard couldn't speak or write a single word of Czech, but he knew exactly what the sign said: "Cellar of the Knights Templar."

In the mid-thirteenth century, the Knights Templar had begun to produce wine in the region. No one knew exactly what had brought them to Čejkovice, or why they had chosen to start growing grapes in the region. The members of the order had built the fortress in Čejkovice and at the same time constructed large cellars—exceptionally large for the day. They were preserved for centuries and further expanded by the Jesuits who settled in Čejkovice, starting in 1623. No information existed today about how big the cellars had originally been.

Rumor had it that the Knights Templar in Čejkovice had had bigger plans than just growing grapes. In his former life as an art thief, grave robber and smuggler, Cloutard had frequently sent teams here to follow up on those stories. But they had found nothing. A rumored labyrinth beneath the Templar fortress, in particular, was supposed to conceal great secrets. People suspected that it had been used by the Templars for storage, and its passageways were said to extend all the way to Skalica, almost fifteen miles away. But until today, no one had found an entrance to the fabled labyrinth. Besides, Cloutard wasn't here for the Knights Templar mythology, but for something else entirely. He was here to grovel.

He found the door that would lead him down to the Templar cellar. He'd seen the man standing guard at the entrance before.

"Is he down below?" Cloutard asked. The man nodded and pointed to the stairs.

Cloutard trotted briskly downstairs, then made his way along a long, narrow corridor lined with enormous wine barrels. They were no ordinary wine barrels, however. The hoops that held the staves together were not, as was usually the case, the same color as the barrel, but practically glowed in the bright red so typical of the Knights Templar. Around half a million liters of wine were stored there. As a wine connoisseur, Cloutard was naturally familiar with the Templar vintages, although South Moravian wines had never really been to his taste. At the end of the corridor, Cloutard saw a man filling a tasting glass with a wine pipette.

"No one who knows you would believe you are here for the wine, Berlin," Cloutard said.

The Welshman turned around slowly and smiled. "It's amazing, isn't it, how often we've crossed paths lately." He filled a second glass and passed it to Cloutard. They raised their glasses in a toast and tasted the wine.

Cloutard frowned, impressed. "*C'est pas mal.* I remembered this wine quite differently," he said.

"Maybe that's because you haven't exactly been rolling in it lately, as they say, and you can't afford the best stuff anymore, *mon ami*," Brice said, with finely tuned sarcasm.

"Touché," Cloutard murmured.

"But you didn't come here just to drink wine with me."

"I could say the same for you. I presume you are still chasing that old Templar stuff? One might think that, sooner or later, you would realize that no Templar treasure exists."

"Of course, François. Just like there's no Sword of Peter, no Ark of the Covenant, no Philosopher's Stone, no Library of Alexandria, and no lost city of Kitezh."

"Touché once more," Cloutard said. He reached for the pipette and filled both glasses a second time.

"What is it you want, Cloutard?"

"I need Karim's papers, the ones you stole from Farid's safe."

"Farid is my business partner, and his wife handed me those documents personally. All proper and correct. I have stolen nothing."

"Call it what you want. But you know as well as I do that the information contained in those papers was the direct result of years of *my* work, and that it belongs to me."

"I can well imagine that it really did take a lot of work. The crème de la crème of art forgers is in there, along with all the museum workers you had on your payroll . . ." The Welshman clucked his tongue. "I'm impressed, François. Even I can learn something from you. But enough beating around the bush. You're not getting your papers back without giving me something in return."

Cloutard sighed. He'd expected nothing else. "What do you want?"

The Welshman strolled over to an old bench beside one of the barrels. A briefcase was lying on top of it. He opened it and took out the file in question. Cloutard's face brightened.

"This thing is so valuable that I actually carry it with me all the time," Brice said, waving the file under Cloutard's nose.

"What do you want for it, Berlin?" He was starting to get annoyed. He didn't like these kinds of games.

"Nothing right now, my friend. But one day, I may want to take advantage of your relationship with Blue Shield for my own ends. And then you will open any door for me that I ask." The Welshman looked at Cloutard with a smug, gloating smile.

Cloutard knew this was his only chance. There was no

point trying to negotiate with the Welshman, and Cloutard was fairly certain he had more than one body-guard with him, so beating him over the head with the pipette and trying to run was not an option either. So he held out his hand. "Good. We have a deal."

Cloutard accepted the file, turned on his heel, and began to leave.

"We'd make a good team, François. Don't you still feel that tingle in your fingers? Have you really decided to follow the straight and narrow, work for starvation wages and put your life on the line for UNESCO?"

Cloutard stopped in his tracks but did not turn back.

"Imagine if you and I had found the artifacts that you discovered with Wagner and Ms. de Mey," Brice continued. "And imagine what that would have meant in sheer wealth for each of us. Now I'm on the trail of another sensational find. You're right: I'm not here for the wine. I'm here for the Chronicle of the Round Table. Think of the power that would give us—and the fortune King Arthur's relics would bring on the black market."

A smile flickered briefly on Cloutard's face. Then he shook his head and left the cellar without another word. He strode back to his car, started the engine, and drove in the direction of Brno. After a few miles, he pulled over and rifled feverishly through the papers, looking for the name Thorvald Brix. It didn't take long to find him, and a few minutes later he had booked a flight from Brno to Copenhagen.

21

ABOVE THE ROOFTOPS OF VENICE

Tom's gun hand began to shake. An eternity seemed to pass, though in reality it was just a few seconds.

Hellen, her father, and Max stared wide-eyed at Tom, as if they were seeing a ghost—which, from their perspective, was the truth. Incomprehension and shock were etched on their faces.

While downstairs, they had seen the old man go up in the elevator and had decided not to wait. A little later—Hellen's voluminous costume slowing them down considerably—they reached the top of the stairs. Standing in front of Lord Whitlock's office, they heard the sounds of a scuffle from inside.

"It's not what it looks like," Tom said, trying to defuse the tension. Slowly, he got to his feet and edged toward the open balcony door. Now was not the time for a reunion or long explanations. The motorcycle guy's lead was growing by the second. Only when Tom reached the window did he realize that he still had the pistol pointed at his friends.

"Sorry," he said, embarrassed, as he stuffed it back under his belt. That was when Max lunged. But he wasn't fast enough. Tom was already through the door and racing along the balcony stretching along the length of the palazzo. He was just in time to see his target climbing around the corner and upped his speed a notch, until he was running as fast as he could. He had to catch the man. Someone outside AF and Blue Shield was also after the Chronicle, and he had to find out who it was. The attacker had had enough time to question Lord Whitlock before Tom had arrived on the scene, and with the lord now dead, the killer was his only lead.

Now, not only did he have to go leaping across the rooftops of Venice like Desmond Miles in "Assassin's Creed," he also had to deal with Max. His former fellow officer had become his pursuer. *Why him?* Tom thought. He couldn't stand Max, and the feeling was mutual.

"Wagner, stop, you're under arrest!" Max shouted behind him. That made Tom smile. Max couldn't possibly believe he'd surrender just because he was shouting at him, could he? Even he couldn't be that stupid. Then again, he'd mispronounced Tom's last name . . .

When Tom reached the end of the balcony, he saw the killer sprinting over the roofs of a lower building along Rio del Vin. He glanced back quickly and saw Max close behind. He would catch up in seconds. Tom looked left and realized that the killer had shimmied down a drainpipe. Tom climbed onto the balustrade and rattled at the pipe. It seemed firmly attached, and he took hold and slid down two floors like a fireman. He landed hard, and tiles on the roof cracked under his feet and slipped away. He almost went with them, but a high chimney stopped him before he tumbled over the edge.

He looked up to see Max just arriving at the end of the balcony—the man was making the chase unnecessarily complicated. Tom picked himself up and ran on. He was lucky: the moon was shining brightly, and he could still see his quarry far ahead. He had turned away to the left, jumping over gables and small skylights, until he came to a stop at the far end of the building, above Calle de le Rasse. The man's hesitation gave Tom a chance to gain a little ground. But the man suddenly backed up a few steps, looked back at Tom, then took off again at full speed and launched himself from the edge of the roof. Seconds later, he disappeared from Tom's field of view.

When Tom reached the spot, with Max still hot on his heels, he realized immediately which way the killer had gone. He jumped and landed on a balcony one floor lower and across the street, rolled and took off again in pursuit of the killer, who had hurled a chair through the balcony door and into the apartment.

The shocked family who lived in the apartment were sitting petrified in front of their TV when Tom zigzagged past them.

"Waaaagggnnneeerrr!" he heard behind him, along with a renewed uproar from the family, as he exited the apartment. *So Max made the jump, too*, he thought. In the stairwell, Tom closed the distance a little, and finally he raced out onto Calle de le Rasse. A quick look left, then right, and Tom had his target back in sight, pushing and shoving his way through the tourists enjoying a romantic evening stroll through Venice.

A couple wheeling their bicycles along the alleyway caught Tom's eye.

"*Missione di Polizia!*" Tom shouted as he pushed the startled man aside and grabbed his bicycle. Seconds later, he was back on the killer's trail, pedaling the bicycle as hard as he could through the narrow alley, shouting and ringing the bell.

22

LORD WHITLOCK'S OFFICE, HOTEL DANIELI

HELLEN HAD HURRIED OUT ONTO THE BALCONY BEHIND Max. She watched, glassy-eyed with shock, as Tom and Max ran. She did not follow them. Her mind was not ready to accept what her senses had just told her.

She had stood over Tom's grave just a few days before, and for a long time before that she had known nothing of his whereabouts. Tom had disappeared, and no one knew what had happened. Then came the news from the U.S. and the sad certainty: Tom was dead. But moments ago he had been standing in front of her, as full of life as ever, and she had watched him kill the one man who could answer their questions about the Templar casket and its contents.

Her mind simply couldn't process it. Deep in shock, she turned back into the room and looked around for somewhere to sit. She felt as if her legs were about to give way. She needed something solid for support. Not only physically, but spiritually. First the worry, then the grief. And now another emotional rollercoaster: suddenly seeing with her own eyes the man, over whose coffin she'd been weeping just days before, alive.

Edward realized immediately the turmoil that must have been going on inside his daughter's head. He took her arm without saying a word, and led her over to an upholstered armchair, where she slumped, exhausted. Her eyes were still locked on the open balcony door. In the lines of her face, Edward could read the struggle she must have been going through and could see how hard it was for her to reconcile what she was feeling with what she had seen.

"He's alive," she whispered, and it sounded to her as if the words were spoken by somebody else. She repeated the words over and over to herself, as if saying them aloud would make it easier to grasp.

Minutes passed, minutes in which her father sat watching her with concern. Minutes in which she just sat there, repeating the words "he's alive" like a mantra. And then, abruptly, her expression changed, as if reason had won out over emotion. Suddenly, she was on her feet and looking firmly at her father.

"We don't have much time. We're in Lord Whitlock's office, and he can't give us any answers anymore. We need to search the place before anyone comes. Maybe we'll find something that will help us further."

Without waiting for her father's reaction, she went over to Lord Whitlock's desk and began to open drawers and sift through the files piled on top.

Edward knew that the subject of Tom's shocking reappearance wasn't closed, but it made no sense to probe any deeper right now. The time for that would come, sooner than Hellen would like. He turned to the bookshelf and began scanning the spines of the books. Most he simply skipped over, until he stopped at an ornate folio with no visible title or author.

Hellen went to Lord Whitlock's body and, nauseated, rifled through his clothes, finding a bunch of keys in the pocket of his trousers. She hurried over to the door and, after a few attempts, found the right one and locked it.

"How are we supposed to find anything here quickly?" she asked with a sigh. Then she turned and saw her father, mesmerized, withdrawing a leather-bound folio from the bookshelf.

23

THE STREETS OF VENICE

Pedestrians jumped clear, screaming and cursing. First, a man in motorcycle leathers had plowed through them recklessly on foot, and moments later another madman was trying to mow them down with a bicycle. A third man was scuffling with a furious walker who was not willing to give up his girlfriend's bike without a fight. Riding bicycles in the old part of Venice was forbidden, and you could only enjoy the miles of bicycle paths after you'd done the right thing and pushed your bicycle out of the center of town—a point that the locals were now making, loudly and with wild gesticulations.

Tom's attempts to clear a path and keep from hurting innocent people by shouting and constantly ringing his bell weren't proving as successful as he had hoped. The narrow alley was lined with small eateries, stores and souvenir shops, and the dodging passersby were stumbling and knocking over chairs and postcard stands on both sides.

The killer turned right at the end of Calle de le Rasse and

sprinted across one of the small bridges that typified Venice. This one crossed the Rio de Palazzo. Artfully worked wall lamps bathed the narrow streets and the waterway in golden light. The man zigzagged quickly through the crowd and disappeared into an alley not much wider than his outstretched arms. Tom was almost on top of him. The long, shallow steps of the bridge barely slowed him down on his bicycle.

"*Polizia, Polizia,*" Tom shouted as he rode. He almost collided with an old woman, but a quick-thinking pedestrian jerked the slow-moving lady out of his path at the last second and Tom was able to swing into the narrow alley.

"Wagner, you asshole! Stop before you kill someone!" Tom suddenly heard behind him. Max had obviously won the battle for the bike and was getting uncomfortably close, which only spurred Tom to pedal harder.

At the end of the alley, the killer sprinted across a small square, passed the Trattoria da Roberto, and turned into Campo San Provolo. Tom was only a few yards behind him now, and he tensed, ready to run the man down at full speed.

But no: there was a dead end ahead. Or was there? Too late, Tom saw that an even smaller connecting passage led onward, hidden behind a blind corner. Sending the bicycle into a sideways skid, he let it fall and went after the killer on foot. Max almost slammed into Tom's fallen bicycle, but managed to come to a stop just in time.

"Halt!" Max bellowed as he also took off into the narrow walkway.

Reaching the other end of the passage, Tom stopped for a moment to try to spot the killer. Which way had he gone? The small bridge to his left was packed with tourists, and the Fondamenta de l'Osmarin led off to the right, running alongside Rio di San Provoio—there, too, it was a busy night. Then Tom spotted the tumult. The killer had crashed into a table at a beer garden, sending drinks and drinkers flying.

As he picked himself up and saw Tom behind him, he made a daring decision. The alley in front of him was getting narrower and narrower, which meant no quick escape that way, and certainly none behind. Instead, he leaped over the iron railing that ran alongside the canal, landing on a moored boat covered with a tarpaulin. From there, he jumped aboard a passing gondola and, with surprising skill, balanced his way back to the stern of the narrow boat.

"*Cacacazzo!*" the gondolier swore as the killer shoved him overboard before jumping to the next boat behind, where he was greeted with similarly colorful language by the gondolier and his guests. The gondolas were lined up one behind the other like links in a chain.

Without the slightest hesitation, Tom followed, barely escaping Max's clutches in the process. Max's fury was written on his face. He hesitated. Then, ignoring every regulation, he decided to continue the pursuit. Tom leaped skillfully from boat to boat, keeping up with the killer. At the next bridge, at the end of Rio de San Provoio —where it opened onto the somewhat wider Rio de San Lorenzo—two police jet skis bobbed at the side of the canal. The killer jumped from the last gondola in the chain onto one of the jet skis and hit the gas.

The two officers in their blue wetsuits and white helmets were just stepping out of a local café, each with an espresso in his hand, when they noticed the commotion in the alley. But they could only stand and watch help-lessly as things happened faster than they could react. Max had gained ground on Tom, and both men were now standing on the same gondola. Max drew his gun.

"Give it up, Wagner. It's the end of the line," Max shouted, but Tom had no intention of just standing there. Max hesitated. Then, like the killer before him, Tom sprang onto the second jet ski and took off in pursuit. He looked back over his shoulder in time to see Max take a bath: Tom's jump had set the gondola rocking violently, and Max lost his balance. Cursing, Max swam back to shore, where he was promptly met by the two astonished water cops.

Tom smiled and opened the throttle wide.

24

LORD WHITLOCK'S OFFICE, HOTEL DANIELI

While Hellen searched frantically through drawers, cupboards and files, Edward was absorbed in the heavy book, scanning every page. Suddenly, he looked up from the ancient folio.

"I don't believe it. The brotherhood is just a legend, surely," he murmured in fascination to himself.

"Which brotherhood?" Hellen asked, but her father didn't answer. Page by careful page, he leafed onward through the book. She snapped her fingers in front of his face.

"Hello! Papa! Which brotherhood are you talking about?" Startled, Edward was seized by a fit of coughing. "Are you all right?"

"It's nothing," he wheezed, recovering himself. "I'm fine. What did you want to know?" he said.

"Which brotherhood?"

"The Society of Avalon," he said with awe.

"Society of Avalon?"

"This book is an old chronicle of a brotherhood that, until today, I'd always thought to be nothing but a legend. In the Arthurian studies that Count Palffy, myself, and a few other colleagues undertook, the name occasionally came up, but we were never able to find any proof that it actually existed," Edward explained, back in the real world again.

"I've never heard of it."

"And no wonder. As I said, the brotherhood is one of history's legendary secrets."

"So what exactly is this 'Society of Avalon'?"

"I'm sure I've told you that the Knights Templar succeeded the Knights of the Round Table, and that the only reason they changed their name was to cover up their past."

"Y-e-e-e-s?" Hellen asked, stretching the word out. She already had an idea where her father was going.

"Well, the Society of Avalon claimed to be the successors to both the Knights Templar and the Knights of the Round Table." Edward laid the folio on the table and pointed to a drawing of a seal. Hellen leaned close and studied the detailed illustration.

"A *croix pattée*, the cross of the Knights Templar," she said in amazement.

"Surrounded by twelve swords." Edward pointed at the star-shaped arrangement of weapons.

"And the dragon in the center . . .?"

"That, my dear, symbolizes King Arthur," Edward said.

Hellen thought silently for a moment. "I know this symbol from somewhere. If only I could remember . . ."

She bent close to the book to decipher the small inscription that bordered the logo. "*Societas Insulae Avaloni*."

'The Society of Avalon,'" Edward translated.

"So it's all true. There really is an order, even today, that succeeded the Knights of the Round Table and the Templars."

"Yes. At least, it looks that way. As I said, it's stories wrapped in myths, the kind of thing you find on conspiracy theory sites on the Internet. As a serious scientist, if you mention things like this at all, it's always done quietly and in private."

"So what are the other myths surrounding these knights? I know you know more than you're telling me!"

"Of course," Edward said with a smile. "The biggest legend of all is the Holy Grail." Hellen's eyes widened. "And everything you think you know about that is completely wrong."

"You mean what Dan Brown said about the Grail wasn't true?" Hellen joked.

"Who?" Edward asked.

"It doesn't matter. Pity. I always thought his theory was very nice," Hellen said, waving it off. "Sorry, what did you want to say?"

"The Knights Templar never found the Holy Grail in Jerusalem, which means they never brought it to Europe."

"No? Then . . . what?"

"The Holy Grail was never actually in the temple in Jerusalem. It was always—"

Suddenly, there was a pounding at the door. Edward and Hellen paled.

"Lord Whitlock?" they heard a worried voice call. The door handle moved as someone tried to open it. More loud knocking. "Are you in there? Is everything all right?"

Hellen recognized the voice of Ruggiero Torrinelli, Whitlock's assistant, who had actually been supposed to accompany them upstairs.

And now they were trapped.

25

THE CANALS OF VENICE

THE COUPLE CLIMBING INTO THEIR BOAT AT THE PRIVATE dock were almost washed away when the killer swung the jet ski hard to the west, sending spray all the way to the second floor. When the wall of chilly water hit the woman, her scream could be heard even over the jet ski's motor.

But there was more to come. When Tom passed a moment later on his 250 HP monster, the couple had not yet managed to get to safety and suffered a second cold shower.

The two jet skis slewed through the narrow waterways. Passing under low bridges, Tom had to duck several times. Moored boats banged against the walls of buildings as they rocked in the wakes of the high-speed chase. Skidding from the Rio della Tetta into the Rio di San Giovanni Laterano, they almost caused an accident: an excursion boat was puttering past the junction just as Tom shot out of the narrow canal. He throttled back instantly, just managing to scrape past the stern of the tourist boat. The killer's lead was narrow, but still big enough for him to roar across the boat's bow. Tom swung his jet ski hard, opened the throttle again, and shot past the long vessel. Two more hard curves and the two machines raced out onto the Grand Canal, or Canałazzo, as the locals called it, and turned to the right. Off to the left, Tom saw the famous Ponte di Rialto footbridge. They swung wide past the boats coming toward them, and bit by bit Tom gained ground. After just over half a mile, the train station appeared on the right. But the killer ignored that, too, and kept going. *Where's he headed?* Tom wondered. A quarter of a mile ahead, the canal made a tight 100-degree turn. But the killer kept going straight ahead, heading for the embankment. When Tom realized what he had in mind, his mind flashed back to his first mission with Hellen, and in his mind's eye he saw again the *grachten*, or canals, of Amsterdam, and the flying motorboats.

Well, then, Tom thought. *It worked the first time . . .*

The two jet skis raced directly toward the small stairway beneath the curve of the Ponte della Costituzione. Harsh scraping and grating and the howling of the engines sent tourists scurrying as the pair of twelve-foot jet skis roared up the steps, one right behind the other. Sparks flew as the they scraped past the pylons of the bridge and ground to a halt. When Tom leaped off his jet ski, the killer was already running up the steps. He continued past the bus station and toward the multistory parking garage across the street. Tom ran as hard as he could. He couldn't let him get away; there was too much at stake. The killer ducked into the garage, then immediately turned left and ran up the spiral ramp. Tom was two steps behind. He reached out for the killer and was just about to tackle him when, as if from nowhere, an SUV careened around a corner and slammed into the killer, catapulting him over the balustrade and three floors straight down.

"My God! I didn't see him!" cried the man who climbed out of the SUV. He ran to the railing and stared down.

"Shit, shit, shit!" Tom muttered. He turned back instantly and ran down again as fast as he could. When he reached the body of the killer, he had to push past the first curious onlookers who had hurried to the man's aid.

"*Polizia!*" Tom shouted, and the people around him made room. "*Chiama medico, chiama medico!*" he yelled at a man standing close by.

A last gurgle escaped the killer's lips as Tom leaned over him. "Who sent you? Who are you working for?" Tom said, shaking at the man's smashed body. But the killer was dead. Tom quickly patted him down, looking for some clue to his identity. On his hand, the man wore a signet ring with an insignia Tom did not recognize: a cross with curving arms of equal length, surrounded by twelve swords arranged in the form of a star. There was an inscription, too: "*Societas Insulae Avaloni.*" In the center of the ring, Tom saw another shield with a cross. Unnoticed, he slipped the ring from the killer's finger and dropped it into his pocket. *Hellen will know something about this*, he thought.

In the inside pocket of the man's jacket, he found a mobile phone and, to his surprise, a mask. He took the mask, then had a closer look at the phone. *Nothing off-*

the-rack, that's for sure, he thought. He placed the man's thumb on the sensor, unlocking it. A picture of Lord Whitlock appeared, and beneath it a note: a date and a few numbers. Tom took out his own phone and photographed the screen, just in case he couldn't unlock the phone later, then put both phones away in his pocket. When the ambulance arrived, Tom exploited the chaos of the growing crowd and slipped away. Back at the Grand Canal, he took a water taxi away from the scene.

26

LORD WHITLOCK'S OFFICE, HOTEL DANIELI

"Goddammit," Hellen whispered.

Edward and Hellen could only stand there, petrified. How were they supposed to explain this? Lord Whitlock lay dead beside his desk, the murder weapon next to him, and Hellen and Edward were in the process of ransacking the office.

"Lord Whitlock?" they heard the assistant's voice call again. The door handle slowly moved up again. Then they heard retreating footsteps and nothing more.

Although they heard Torrinelli walking away, they barely dared to breathe. They stood that way for several minutes, not moving an inch.

"We have to get this folio out of here," Hellen finally whispered, breaking the silence.

"But how?" Edward asked. "It's a little too big to tuck under our clothes."

"Maybe I can help."

Hellen and Edward turned around in alarm. Tom Wagner, his hands raised, stepped out from behind the billowing curtain over the balcony door. Hellen turned chalk-white. She had pushed aside the fact that she had seen a ghost not even an hour earlier. For a moment, all three just stood and stared at each other. Then Hellen ran to Tom, threw her arms around him, and hugged him as tightly as she could.

"Hellen," Tom stammered, hardly able to breathe, holding her just as tightly. Finally, they were together again. They stood in each other's arms for a long time before they separated, only for Hellen to look deep into Tom's eyes.

"It's really you."

"Yes, and I'm so s—"

But that was as far as he got, because Hellen had taken a step back and slapped him as hard as she could across his face.

"Where the hell have you been? I was sick with worry, and after Cloutard scoured heaven and earth for you we got a cryptic message from the States that you'd died." Hellen's eyes filled with tears, and she paced distraught through the room. "All of us . . . we . . . I . . . how is this even possible?" She stopped and stared at him. "You're alive." Shaking her head, she went back to him and threw her arms around him a second time, sobbing helplessly, clawing her fingers into his back.

"I am so, so sorry. I didn't want . . ." But he broke off, pulled her close and kissed the top of her head.

Suddenly, she began pounding wildly against his chest. "Where were you? I went to your fucking funeral!" She let him go again, hastily wiping the tears from her eyes, and gradually managed to get herself back under control. "What happened? Where have you been all this time?" she asked, her voice calmer.

Tom hesitated. There was no way he could tell her where he'd really been and what he'd had to do, let alone for whom he was now being forced to work. That was part of the deal he'd made with Ossana, and the price for Hellen's father's life. Tom looked across at Edward, then back at Hellen.

"I can't tell you the details . . ." Hellen's eyes narrowed. Edward was standing beside his daughter now, and he placed one arm around her shoulders. "All I can tell you is that it had to do with my uncle and the CIA."

"The CIA? Why in God's name are you mixed up with the CIA?"

"I promise you, when the time comes, I'll tell you everything, but for now I need you to trust me."

Hellen nodded, not entirely convinced.

"And what did you have to do with this?" Edward said, and he pointed to the body of Lord Whitlock.

"It wasn't me," Tom said, raising his hands defensively. "My assignment was—" But he cut himself short. "I was supposed to talk to him, but when I came in there was a guy already here. I don't know why he was here—maybe to interrogate or kidnap Lord Whitlock?—but I walked into the middle of it. We fought and he shot Whitlock, and when you walked in," he nodded toward Hellen and Edward, "the killer ran, and I went after him." He pointed toward the balcony.

Hellen and Edward shared a rather incredulous glance.

Tom took out the ring from inside his jacket. "I found this on him." He held the ring up for them to see.

Father and daughter looked at each other in delight. Slowly, hesitantly, still not entirely sure he was real, Hellen approached Tom. Her eyes were fixed on the ring. She took it and turned it over in her hand, examining it closely. Suddenly she was back to her old self. Excited and bubbling over with enthusiasm, she turned to her father.

"Now I remember! The old priest, in Glastonbury, what was his name again?" She snapped her fingers, searching her memory. "Father Montgomery. He had a ring just like this."

"You mean the priest who gave you the clue about the Meteora monastery? What does he have to do with this?" Tom frowned deeply. Surely there couldn't be a connection.

"Yes, him, exactly," Hellen said. "Glastonbury fits the picture perfectly."

Edward took the ring now and read the inscription on it. "Societas Insulae Avaloni—the Society of Avalon really exists," he breathed, hardly able to believe his own words.

"The Society of what now?"

27

RUGGIERO TORRINELLI'S OFFICE, HOTEL DANIELI

TORRINELLI MIGHT HAVE BEEN MISTAKEN, BUT HE COULD have sworn he had heard a female voice inside the office.

It was not at all out of character for Lord Whitlock to retire to his office and shut out the world around him. Sometimes he would lock himself away for days, forgetting even to eat.

But if he's not in his office, where the devil is the old fart, Torrinelli thought. *Did he change his mind and go back to the party after all?* That seemed unlikely. Torrinelli went to his own office, at the end of the hallway, and closed the door behind him. No one could be allowed to see what he was about to do. The hotel security guards and staff— and Lord Whitlock himself—took privacy very seriously. This would be an unforgivable breach.

He sat down at his desk, opened his laptop and put on a pair of Bluetooth headphones. Four surveillance cameras, from four different perspectives, transmitted crystal-clear images from Lord Whitlock's office straight to his monitor. Of course, the old man had no clue the cameras even existed.

When Torrinelli had started his job as Whitlock's assistant, he had thrown himself into it heart and soul. He had just graduated from Università di Firenze, and could not believe his luck when he got the opportunity to work for the old man. But Lord Whitlock was a secretive bastard, and Torrinelli quickly realized the sobering truth: Whitlock would never share any of his really exciting discoveries with him.

His day-to-day work consisted of the kinds of boring tasks better suited to a museum attendant. Sometimes he got the feeling that Lord Whitlock only put up with him because he was the size of a refrigerator. He was much more a bodyguard than an assistant. And to add insult to injury, the pay was terrible. Whitlock was every bit as tight-fisted as Scotsmen were said to be. After a couple of years, when Torrinelli realized he was never going to be given either more responsibility or a better salary, he drew the obvious conclusion: it was time to look for a second source of income. And he found it, with someone who was both willing both to pay him handsomely for his services and who also saw in him an investment in the future. All of which had led Torrinelli, one quiet day, to secretly bug his boss's office with sound and video. Ever since, Lord Whitlock's every move was recorded 24/7, and Torrinelli reported regularly to his new patron.

I knew I heard a voice. It's that woman, Hellen de Mey, Torrinelli thought, listening closely to every word they said. But where was Lord Whitlock? His question was answered seconds later when the young woman stepped aside to reveal the old man's body.

"Fuck! They've whacked Whitlock!" Torrinelli exclaimed, unable to conceal his smile. *Well, at least I've been spared that shitty job*, he thought. His client had already made it known that, sooner or later, Whitlock would have to go. Adrenalin suddenly pumping, he continued to listen.

28

LORD WHITLOCK'S OFFICE, HOTEL DANIELI

"THE SOCIETY OF AVALON," EDWARD REPEATED. "BUT telling you all that would take too long right now." Edward stepped toward Tom and held out his hand. "I'm Edward de Mey, by the way. Hellen's father."

"Pleased to meet you. Tom Wagner, Hellen's . . ." He hesitated.

"Colleague," Hellen said, with an uncertain glance at Tom.

"Yes. We work—uh, used to work—together," Tom said, somewhat confused.

The situation was starting to get embarrassing, and Hellen quickly changed the subject. "So what have you done with my *new* colleague?"

Tom's eyes opened wide and pointed at his own chest. "Who, me? To Max? Nothing, I swear. He went for a swim somewhere."

"And it wasn't you who sent him for a swim?"

"Even if it was, I had a killer to catch, and that idiot was just in the way. How did you end up with a mouth-breather like him, anyway?" Hellen was about to answer when Tom interrupted. "Wait, let me guess: Maierhofer put his 'best man' at your disposal. Competent and follows orders. A real team player," Tom said with a smirk, mimicking Maierhofer's voice. Hellen nodded and rolled her eyes. "I'm glad you were able to replace me so quickly. Really makes a guy feel appreciated." He sighed theatrically, but quickly grew serious again. "I found something else, too." Tom took out his phone and showed them the picture he'd taken of the killer's phone display.

"The killer was sent for Whitlock, no question about it," he continued. "And if you ask me, he was here to kidnap him. This shows a date and coordinates. On the taxi ride here, I checked out the coordinates. It's somewhere in the Italian Alps. That's my next stop. What are you going to do now?"

"Let's talk about it later," said Edward. "We need to get out of here as fast as we can. Next time, his assistant isn't just going to knock. And I'd prefer to be gone when that happens."

"Good idea," said Hellen.

"Then after you, Your Majesty." Tom stepped aside, bowed before Hellen in her imperial outfit, and ushered her toward the balcony.

"And how do you see this working?" She shook her head with a frown and indicated her enormous hoop skirt.

"Can't you just climb out of there and toss it in a corner somewhere?" Tom replied, grinning broadly.

"He's right, Hellen. This really isn't the time for false modesty." Edward began to loosen the straps at Hellen's back, and she slipped out of the red top, petticoat and hoop skirt.

Tom's grin only widened. Hellen was standing in front of him clothed only in a tight corset and Lolita bloomers.

"I'm going to freeze my butt off out there," Hellen said.

"I wouldn't worry too much about your enchanting butt." Tom's eyes were glued to Hellen's generous cleavage as he slipped out of his jacket and offered it to her.

Edward cleared his throat.

"Children, can we get a move on?"

Tom and Hellen nodded and, for a moment, looked deep into each other's eyes. Then they ran out onto the balcony and down to the end.

"We still have to get our things from the room and change," Edward said. "It's just below us, one floor down."

Tom sighed. "All right, but we have to hurry. Once they find Whitlock's body, all hell's going to break loose. We want to be far away from here by then."

Using the same drainpipe as before, they climbed down to the balcony below.

"Really though, what did you do with Max?" Hellen asked.

"Nothing. Cross my heart."

"I'm going to call him, otherwise all I'm going to hear from Mother is that we're not allowed to make another move without him. He's supposed to be looking after us," Hellen said, as she listened to the phone ring. "Voicemail," she said, clicking off the call.

"I've found him," said Tom, and he pointed through the window into the hotel room the three of them shared. Tom knocked on the glass and Max jumped in alarm. He'd only just gotten back to the room himself and had just pulled down his trousers.

"Max," Hellen whispered, waving him over.

Amazed, Max pulled up his pants again and opened the balcony door, but his expression changed the moment Tom stepped into the room. He barged at him and swung a right cross, but Tom dodged easily. Edward grabbed hold of Max and held him back.

"Easy, Max. It's okay. He's on our side," Hellen said.

"Did you know that swimming in the canals is illegal?" Max said indignantly, holding a citation in the air. "That's going on my expense account."

Hellen had to laugh.

"What happens now?" Tom asked.

"You and I," Edward said, swinging his arm around Tom and squeezing him harder than necessary, "are going to pick up the trail in Italy so I can get to know my daughter's 'colleague' a little better, while Hellen and Max follow up on the dead priest in Glastonbury. Sound like a plan?"

————

"Mr. Brice, I have some good news," said Ruggiero Torrinelli when he got the Welshman was on the phone.

"I'm all ears," Brice said.

"To start with: the bounty you put on Hellen de Mey? You can send it to the usual account. I know exactly where she is, and I also know where she's going," Torrinelli said smugly, and he swung the hotel surveillance camera across the plaza to where Hellen, Edward, Tom and Max were leaving the hotel and climbing into a water taxi.

29

ROYAL LIBRARY, COPENHAGEN, DENMARK

CLOUTARD CLIMBED OUT OF A TAXI AND LOOKED UP AT THE "Black Diamond," as the ultramodern extension of Denmark's national library was known. The edifice's futuristic, Cubist design was realized in polished black stone imported from Zimbabwe. It had been built to provide the space needed to house the largest collection of books in northern Europe: five million volumes and fifteen million manuscripts were kept on one hundred miles of shelving.

There was probably no library that Cloutard knew better, because what had happened here at the end of the 1960s and the beginning of the 70s had had a major influence on the course of his life. As a ten-year-old, he had heard for the first time about the biggest book theft in history: over ten years, more than 3200 historical works worth almost 40 million euros were stolen, among them manuscripts from Martin Luther and original works by Immanuel Kant, Thomas More, and John Milton. Nobody had even noticed anything was missing until

1975. In the following decades, the stolen works were sold at auction—sometimes publicly through houses like Sotheby's and Christie's, sometimes on the black market —and Cloutard's foster father had told him about it in great detail.

The crime had been carried out by an employee of the library, completely unaided, for years, and was only discovered after he died. His family, who knew about it, had not been careful enough when trying to sell a number of the stolen works.

Young François had been so fascinated by the case that he had made up his mind to become an art thief. Inspired by the Copenhagen case, Cloutard had turned away from the family business. At first, his foster father— the head of an Italian Mafia family—couldn't accept it at all. But when, some years later, Cloutard showed him the kind of numbers he was working with, the aging don was forced to revise his opinion of his foster son's art-world dealings.

And Cloutard was also struck by the irony that not only had the greatest art-related theft in history taken place in this library, but that it was also where the best living counterfeiter of artworks pursued his profession as a librarian. No one suspected Thorvald Brix of anything.

The Frenchman glared at the modern library building. He found it hideous. Cloutard was an aesthete who had little time for modern art, architecture or music. He thought momentarily about what modernism had done to the art of cooking, physically shuddering when he thought of the monstrosities created in the name of "molecular cuisine." In his mid-fifties, Cloutard was not exactly the most open-minded of men. He was a lover of classical art, good manners, and the lifestyles of bygone days, and—true to his tastes—he decided to enter the library via the older part of the complex.

Directly connected to the "Black Diamond" and standing in stark contrast to it was the original building, dating from 1673 and in continuous use to the present day. It had been built in imitation of the architectural style of medieval northern Italy and the early Renaissance, with Venetian accents, and bore similarities with the Charlemagne Chapel in Aachen Cathedral in Germany. Cloutard sighed with satisfaction. Crossing the Christiansborg courtyard, he turned into Det Kongelige Biblioteks Have, the park in front of the red brick building. With its ponds and fountains, the park had a reputation as the most peaceful place in downtown Copenhagen.

Cloutard bought a ticket, entered the library, and made his way through the countless corridors and levels to one of the old-style reading rooms: green marble columns, shelves and reading desks of ancient oak, high arches, classical emerald-green reading lamps, and real daylight pouring in from three sides of the hall. Cloutard loved the magic of libraries, the accumulation of knowledge and old, priceless assets in the form of books, folios, manuscripts and codices.

He spotted Brix at the far end of the room. He was an unassuming man of about sixty, pushing a book cart ahead of him and returning books to bookshelves at a snail's pace. Cloutard had moved through the room silently, and no one had taken any notice of him. All had their noses in their books.

Cloutard made it to within a few steps of Brix when the librarian suddenly turned and saw him. Brix's face froze. He screamed in horror, pushed the book cart at Cloutard, and began to run. The cart tipped over, and dozens of books landed at Cloutard's feet. The people studying in the reading room jumped, startled, and turned to see Brix running away. Cloutard clambered over the pile of books and took up the chase, accompanied by a chorus of shushing and indignant tirades. Brix was out of the reading room now and running along the corridor, but it very quickly became clear that his escape attempt was in vain. Apart from forging paintings, his lifelong work at the library was all the exercise he got. He quickly ran out of breath, and Cloutard caught up.

"I didn't have anything to do with it," was the first thing he said. "It wasn't my idea. I didn't know you were going to get ripped off," he stammered, gasping for air between words. The twenty-second sprint had clearly sapped his strength, and only now did Cloutard realize why Brix had run at all.

"*Mon ami*, if you are talking about the old Campendonk picture, don't worry. I forgot all about that long ago. Forget it. We almost got caught, but in the end it was only almost."

Brix's face began to relax a little, although he was still terribly out of breath. "Then what do you want from me, François? Back then you wanted forgeries worth millions."

Cloutard looked around. People were walking by. He leaned close to Brix and whispered, "What do you think I want? I need your artistic talents."

By the time they reached the garden, Cloutard had outlined the scope of the project to the counterfeiter.

Brix grinned broadly. "Exciting stuff. But very complicated, too. I'm going to need an incredible amount of material, and I can't just conjure it out of thin air. The gold leaf alone . . ."

Cloutard smiled and was about to answer when Brix stopped him. "And if you're planning to tell me that this commission will make us square, forget it. The materials I'm talking about aren't easy to obtain. I have my sources, of course, but if you need it fast, it's going to cost you."

Cloutard raised his eyebrows in a frustrated frown as they crossed the courtyard of Christiansborg Palace. "How much, exactly?"

"I'm talking in the high six figures, just for the material. And yes, you'll have to pay me, too, so best make it seven digits. But that shouldn't be a problem for you, should it?"

My God! Brix is the only man in the business who does not know that I am broke yet, Cloutard thought. *And it is better if it stays that way*. "Of course it is not a problem," he said, trying to sound as convincing as possible.

"And you'll pay for the travel and my accommodation."

Cloutard knew instantly what he meant.

"You know I need a certain environment around me to be able to work well. If you have no objections, I'll leave tomorrow. I'll need a few days to settle in. The materials can be there within 24 hours."

Cloutard began to add up what it would all cost, and his forehead began to perspire despite the chill in the Copenhagen air. But he managed to nod again as if it made no difference at all. "Of course, *mon ami*. I will get the money and we will meet in Sorrento."

Thorvald Brix's face brightened when he heard the name of the city on the Gulf of Naples where he had produced all of his most important forgeries. But Cloutard's heart sank. It wouldn't be easy to put together that kind of money in such a short time.

30

AOSTA VALLEY, ITALIAN ALPS

TOM AND EDWARD LEFT THE TOWN OF BREUIL BEHIND them, Tom guiding the rented IVECO Massif up the winding mountain road toward Plan-Maison-Cervena. The small skiing village lay shrouded in fog at an altitude of around 6,500 feet in the Aosta Valley, below the Matterhorn in the Italian Alps.

"Not far now," Edward said with a glance at the GPS.

"I'm curious about what's waiting for us in the middle of a ski resort," Tom said.

"Well, in about eight miles we'll find out."

Despite the masses of snow, the 4x4 ground its way up the idyllic mountain road. The only other vehicles on the road were the occasional tour bus, working hard to make any headway even with snow chains. But they were few and far between; heavy snowfall, icy winds, and fog could deter even the hardiest skier.

"Tom, I'm asking you again not to say a word about my illness to my daughter. It was one of the reasons I came back, but even so, I don't want Hellen to spend the little time she and I have left worrying about me."

"You can count on me, Doc. My lips are sealed." Tom nodded understandingly and hoped that was the end of the matter, at least until he completed his mission and could finally tell his side of the story. All the secretiveness was starting to get to him. It was different when the people he had to lie to weren't his friends.

On the flight from Venice to Milan, Edward had talked expansively about the Knights of the Round Table, King Arthur and the Knights Templar, bringing Tom up to speed. But during the drive up into the mountains, to Tom's irritation, the conversation had turned to far more personal matters. He felt like he was being interrogated. He'd been compelled to reveal his relationship to Hellen, which was far from simple and a topic he was reluctant to talk about with Hellen's father. After a few fatherly words of advice and the obligatory warnings from a concerned father had come the revelation: Edward had told Tom about his incurable disease.

"Thank you," Edward said now. "Hellen has enough on her plate already just trying to deal with your resurrection."

Tom swallowed and forced a smile. "It's like I said: the day will come when I can explain everything that's happened," he replied, trying to ignore the barb from Hellen's father.

"The summit station should be just ahead," Edward said. "We should be able to get a good view from there."

Moments later, the Hotel Stambecco appeared atop a small plateau. Tom parked the car. Icy wind whipped around their ears when they left the cozy warmth of the Massif. Tom pulled up the fake-fur-lined hood of his parka and reached for the binoculars on the back seat. Then the two men hurried around the hotel, heading for the viewing platform, which turned out to be devoid of other people except for one hardened man whose nicotine addiction was enough to get him out on to the platform even in this weather. The platform normally offered a panoramic view of the valley below, where the small reservoir of Lago Goillet lay. But the visibility was terrible, not helped at all by the heavy snowfall. Tom turned the binoculars toward the lake.

"I can hardly see a thing," he muttered, sweeping the lake from one end to the other. But then he spotted the vague outline of a small house to the southeast of the reservoir. Two SUVs were parked in front of it, and a handful of men in military winter fatigues were patrolling nearby.

"I think we're in the right place," Tom said, and he handed the field glasses to Edward.

"That's gotta be some kind of military site, right?" the apparently tipsy American suddenly said, having stepped up beside Tom and Edward. His unmistakable accent and his appearance betrayed his origins. "You want to know what I think? I think they're hidin' secret labs beneath the dam wall. You know, for aliens or somethin'."

Edward and Tom looked at each other in surprise and had to bite their lips to keep from laughing out loud.

"Take my word for it, strange things are happenin' down there. You gentlemen wanna have a drink wi' me?" Swaying a little, the man took a hip flask from beneath his ski jacket and offered it to Tom and Edward.

"No thanks," Tom said, and Edward just shook his head.

"Fucking snobs," the man said with a shrug. "Well, all the more for me." He took a slug and wiped his mouth contentedly with his glove before putting the flask away again in his jacket. "Gotta numb the pain somehow. You can't ski in this shitty weather, and you can't relax with all the racket."

"What racket?" Edward asked in surprise, lowering the binoculars.

"The chopper. Every two hours, this monster chopper flies right through here, disappears behind the Matterhorn, then comes back a while later and lands down there at the dam. I'm tellin' you, somethin's goin' on down there."

Edward peered through the binoculars again and shook his head imperceptibly.

"It's probably just some super-rich guys getting flown in to heliski," Tom said, wanting to get rid of the conspiracy-theorist drunk.

"Excuse us." Edward grabbed Tom by his arm and pulled him aside. "Someone's coming." He handed Tom the binoculars and pointed down to the lake.

A third SUV came bumping along the road and pulled up beside the others. A man climbed out, and before he could throw his hood over his head, Tom was able to see that he was wearing a mask—the same mask that Tom had found on the killer in Venice. When one of the soldiers came to the man, he raised his hand flat in front of his eyes, paused like that for a moment, then flipped his hand up as if he were opening the visor of a helmet. A greeting? Tom had once read that modern military salutes had evolved from the days of the knights, because when knights met that lifted their visors in greeting.

"They're wearing masks," Tom said. Edward's brow furrowed and he thought for a moment.

"Then maybe the ring is a form of identification. If every ring has a different shield in the center, then the members of the Society of Avalon could identify each other and still remain anonymous."

"I'm starting to feel like I'm in a bad spy movie," Tom joked. "Then again, why not? If you think about it, it's pretty damn smart. No one knows who anyone is, so none of them can blow the whistle on any of the others." Tom returned his gaze to the binoculars. "And we have a way in. We have the ring, and we have this, too." Tom fished out the mask that he'd taken from the killer and handed it to Edward.

"And what's my role in your crazy plan?"

"Milord, it's time for you to discover your inner noble-man. That's why the killer was in Venice: he was going to kidnap Lord Whitlock and bring him here. And that's exactly what we're going to do." He slipped the ring onto his right hand and glanced at the insignia.

As they made their way back to the car, they heard the distant roar of a helicopter that had just appeared over the summit of the Matterhorn. Tom raised the binoculars again to get a closer look at the huge white machine. *That guy was right*, he thought as the chopper flew over them and headed straight for the dam.

"We're definitely in the right place. It's an AgustaWest-land AW101, aka 'Merlin'."

Tom climbed into the car, starting to feel motivated, and looked across at Edward, who seemed far less happy about his role in their plan. Tom turned the car around and drove.

31

GLASTONBURY, SOMERSET COUNTY, ENGLAND

HELLEN HAD BEEN THINKING ABOUT IT FOR THE ENTIRE flight and had even grown a little frightened. And now that she was back, everything came crashing down on her like a wave. This is where it had all begun. This was where she had found the very first clue, here in Glastonbury. All of the adventures with Tom and Cloutard had followed from that. And now, standing with Max in the parking lot in front of Glastonbury Abbey, she again felt the strange energy of the place. It wasn't just that King Arthur and his wife, Queen Guinevere, were said to be buried there. Glastonbury was actually claimed by some to be the legendary Avalon, around which the myths of Merlin, the Grail, Excalibur, Tristan's love potion, and the adventures of Sir Lancelot seemed to circle.

But there was something else that made Avalon special: one of the ley lines that spanned the globe passed directly through Glastonbury. In the 19th century, a number of writers had started using the term "ley lines" to describe the way that landmarks such as megaliths, ancient places of worship, and churches seemed to be geographically arranged in straight lines. And even though many of those ideas had been debunked in the years since, Glastonbury had lost none of its magic—because of the most fascinating legend of all.

"So are we hunting for the Holy Grail now?" Max said, after Hellen had spent the flight telling him everything she knew about Glastonbury. He could hardly have been more bored or irritated. He really had no interest in old artifacts and the fascinating stories behind them ... after all, he wasn't Tom. But since Tom had resurfaced, he'd certainly seemed to her to be acting a little suspicious. She didn't think that he was up to no good, of course, but something odd lay between them.

"No. Not directly, anyway. The legend that Joseph of Arimathea brought certain sacred relics here was introduced by the French poet Robert de Boron in his version of the Grail story in the early 13th century. They believe he actually wrote a trilogy, but only fragments of his later works have survived to the present day. Still, his work was the inspiration for the subsequent Vulgate Cycle of Arthurian history."

Max, overwhelmed by too much information, looked away and puffed out his cheeks. Too many names, too many facts for his soldier's brain to handle. Hellen had always thought that Tom had nothing in his head but action and adrenaline, but at the time she hadn't met Max. She decided to tune out his boredom. It felt good to her to talk about these things a little.

"De Boron wrote that Joseph caught the blood of Jesus in a goblet, the Holy Grail, and that the Grail was later brought to Britain. But the trail, of course, vanishes here."

Max looked toward the ruins of the abbey, the original form of which could only be guessed at from the few remaining walls and arches scattered around the extensive grounds. "It's just a pile of old rocks," he said, and the words were like a knife to Hellen's heart. She could not understand how anyone could be so oblivious to the energy emanating from this magical place.

She shook her head and gave up trying to get Max even a little bit interested in history. "I don't actually know what we're looking for," she said. "All I know is that the last time I was here, Father Montgomery was wearing the same ring that Lord Whitlock's killer was wearing."

"So we're going to visit this priest?"

"No. Father Montgomery was murdered. He died in my arms." Hellen sighed and wiped away a tear. "I didn't really consciously notice his ring at the time, because I had other things on my mind. Come with me. We have to visit St. Margaret's Chapel."

They took the same route that Hellen had followed a year before, following Magdalena Street past a shop called The Startled Hare Antiques & Curiosities before turning left into a narrow lane that led into what was known as the "quiet garden." Hellen felt a chill as she entered. It wasn't because of the damp, chilly British winter, however, but because of the memories that came flooding back. This was where she had found the priest, whose dying act had been to give her the clue about

Meteora, the legendary monastery in Greece that, soon after, had become the scene of a massacre.

Max, of course, noticed nothing. He crept through the garden like a member of a SWAT team about to storm a building in New York, living up to every cliché in the book.

"It's late. I don't think there'll be anybody here," he said.

Wow. I'm so glad he figured that out. What a whiz, Hellen thought. She already knew what they had to do.

"We're going to break into the sacristy," she said matter-of-factly. She smiled at the role reversal. Suddenly, she was the reckless one, the daredevil. *All that time around Tom*, she thought.

She pointed to the door visible on the right of the garden. Straight ahead lay the small chapel where Father Montgomery had died.

"Can you give that a solid kick, please?" she said, pointing at the door.

Max looked at her indignantly but did as she asked. Hellen stepped into the small room.

"Everything looks just like it did then," she murmured. On that terrible day, she had spent a long time waiting in the sacristy before the police arrived, passing the time by looking over the books stored in the small bookcase. Nothing seemed to have changed at all. She paused, though, when the titles of a series of books caught her eye. She had seen them a year ago, but hadn't ascribed any particular significance to them at the time. She had been looking for very different clues.

She quickly pulled the books from the bookshelf and sat down with them at the small desk. Max watched, and the glimmer of a smile crossed his face—when she was as deeply enthralled in something as she was now, she had a very special radiance. And she was an exceptionally good-looking woman, a fact that Max seemed to notice now for the first time. Giving in to her attraction, he sat on the edge of the desk, feigning interest in what she'd found.

"This is part of the series known as the 'Bibliothèque de la Pléiade.' It contains the entire Vulgate Cycle, the origin of the Holy Grail legend."

"Well, that *is* interesting," Max said, and he leaned closer. Hellen raised her eyebrows in surprise but returned her attention to the books and began leafing quickly through the pages of the three-volume "Le Livre du Graal." The books were a new English translation published at the start of the 2000s, which made them a lot easier to read than 12th century Old French would have been.

"The first volume is about Joseph, the second about Lancelot, and in the third he talks about the Grail and the death of King Arthur."

She knew, of course, that it made no sense to try and read the books there and then. They were probably available digitally, anyway, and she could sit and give them her undivided attention online. She was about to put the books away again when she noticed a few handwritten notes. Someone had been writing in the margins of the pages, and that meant that she definitely had to take a closer look. Decision made: she would take the books with her.

"What are you doing in here?"

The sudden voice almost gave her a heart attack.

A man had entered the sacristy and was looking at them wide-eyed. The look on his face, however, was surpassed by the look on Max's. He had been so busy inching closer to Hellen that his vigilance had failed miserably.

"Aren't you a great lookout," Hellen muttered to Max. But she knew the new arrival: in front of her stood no less than the young priest she'd asked for help the last time she was here, when she had found Father Montgomery's body. And the young priest recognized her, too.

"Ms. de Mey? What are you doing here?" His face relaxed.

"I'm here on a new project. It's extremely urgent, so I hope you'll excuse us forcing our way in. In my research, I stumbled across a signet ring, and I recalled that Father Montgomery also wore the same kind of ring. Do you remember it?"

Hellen hoped fervently that the priest wouldn't ask questions about the break-in.

"I do, actually. But—"

Hellen's phone rang just then, interrupting the priest. She glanced at it. "Excuse me. It's important." She stood up and left the sacristy, walking out to the small courtyard.

The young priest, who rarely had to deal with women as

strong-willed as Hellen, did not protest. Hellen took the call, and her expression clouded over. She nodded a few times, then hung up and returned to the two men.

"That was Vittoria. Our two Blue Shield colleagues in Istanbul have been found dead. She wants to follow it up on her own," she said to Max.

The young priest crossed himself. Hellen turned to face him. "Back to us." Hellen's voice had gotten a notch sharper—another thing she had picked up from Tom. Self-confidence was the key: lie like you mean it and you'll get away with it nearly every time. "I'm sorry, but I've said all I can about why we're here. Except this: we've come in the name of the Vatican," she lied smoothly. "Please don't ask any more questions or you'll put me in an uncomfortable position. Can we count on your support?"

Max struggled to keep a straight face.

The priest nodded and gave Hellen a restrained smile. "After Father Montgomery's death, they went through his room. Everything he owned was carted off to London. He's buried there, in Charlton Cemetery." The young man crossed himself again.

"To London?"

"Yes. As far as I know, everything is with the Seraphim."

32

LAGO GOILETT, MOUNTAIN LAKE IN THE ITALIAN ALPS

"I KNOW I'M GOING TO DIE SOON, BUT I'M NOT ENTIRELY sure I want to speed the process up," said Edward when Tom suddenly stopped the car half a mile from their destination.

"Stay calm, we can do it," Tom said, trying to calm Hellen's father, and he climbed out of the car.

"What are you going to do?" asked Edward, following Tom around to the trunk.

"You're my prisoner, and it has to look like it. Here, pull that over your head." Tom handed him the black cloth bag from the binoculars. Then he opened the rear doors of the SUV and gestured invitingly.

"Are you serious?" Edward asked, but he reluctantly climbed inside.

"Give me your hands."

Edward stopped Tom before he tied him up. "Aren't you afraid they're going to recognize you despite the mask?"

Tom thought for a moment. "No, actually. The guy I was trying to catch in Venice was very similar to me in build, and we had almost the same hair color. The mask will take care of the rest."

"And your voice? How do you know he wasn't from Iceland and had a terrible accent?"

"Okay, fine, there's still some risk. But he was most likely British, right?"

"You're gambling for high stakes. But if my daughter trusts you, then I can, too." Edward reached out his hands again for Tom to tie.

"Don't worry." He bound Edward's hands with a cable tie, pulled the bag over his face, and slammed the doors.

"If I don't get out of this alive, Hellen's never going to forgive you, you know," Edward shouted as Tom, behind the wheel again, pulled back onto the road.

"That's my job. Nothing's going to happen to you, trust me. Comfortable back there?"

It wasn't only Edward who was nervous. Tom's own adrenaline level was rising. They were driving straight into the lion's den. Only a few dozen yards separated them now from the house. Off to the left stood the mighty helicopter, its spinning blades stirring up a small snow squall. Tom turned off the ignition and climbed out as a soldier approached. As he'd seen another man do earlier, he saluted in greeting, presenting the ring in the process.

"You're late, Galahad. Why the delay?" the soldier yelled to make himself heard over the noise from the chopper. The man's face was hidden behind ski goggles and a face mask. A tactical helmet and snow camouflage gear rounded out the high-tech soldier look. He carried a Heckler & Koch assault rifle slung over his shoulder. Tom went around the car and opened the back of the SUV.

The moment of truth had arrived. Tom cleared his throat and hoped that his British accent didn't sound too amateurish.

"This is why. My assignment was to bring this man here. He got a little unruly on the way," Tom shouted back as he helped Edward out of the back.

Without another word, the soldier led them to the heli-copter. Bent low, with their hands up to protect them-selves from the icy wind driven by the rotors, the three men made their way to the rear hatch of the helicopter. Tom led Edward inside and the hatch closed behind them. There was no turning back now.

Two soldiers removed the chocks blocking the heli-copter's wheels. A third signaled to the pilot to lift off.

Tom and Edward moved through the luxurious cabin. Tom had not expected to see such opulence in a heli-copter like this. It was more like the interior of a private jet or the U.S. president's chopper, Marine One. He pushed Edward roughly onto a vacant leather chair and sat down beside him. There was only one other person in the cabin with them, sitting on the starboard side, his face also hidden behind a mask. The man raised his arm in an indifferent greeting and returned his attention to his laptop. Tom returned the greeting. He had recognized the man's ring instantly. It was the same as his, but with one difference: as far as Tom could see, his bore the coat of arms of Lancelot. On their flight here, Edward had inducted him into the legends surrounding King Arthur.

Looks like I wasn't the only one running late, Tom thought. He scanned the cabin, which was completely fitted out in beige leather and walnut paneling. All of the Knights of the Round Table would have fit inside there easily. The engines howled, and the giant machine slowly lifted off. Tom looked out the window and watched as they quickly gained altitude and then turned and headed straight for the Matterhorn. Once they passed the summit, the helicopter swung in a wide curve and descended toward the glacier that seemed to swell out of a circular recess in the side of the mountain, about half a mile across.

"No way," Tom whispered, careful not to reveal his astonishment to his fellow passenger. "There's a castle down there, on a rocky ridge in the middle of the glacier," he whispered in Edward's ear. Edward sat unmoving in his leather seat, presumably sick with fear, and awaited his fate.

The helicopter came down to land on a rocky plateau opposite the castle, settling back to earth with a gentle jolt. Lancelot packed his laptop away, stood up, and waited for the rear hatch to open.

"We're here. On your feet," Tom said harshly to Edward. He grabbed him by the arm and pulled him out of the machine, Edward stumbling along beside him. The pilot shut down the engines and the rotors slowed to a stop.

Tom's amazement only grew as they drew closer to the castle and he saw just how magnificent it was. Rough-hewn stone, white towers with pointed, snow-covered roofs, and an immense door. Unbelievable. They were almost 10,000 feet above sea level, and Tom was staring at a medieval castle. For a moment, a tinge of sadness came over him: Hellen would have loved it.

"Doc, you're not going to believe this."

A stone bridge led from the rocky plateau they had landed on across a small chasm and directly to the door of the imposing structure. The glacier curved in a graceful sweep around the bridge's pylons and continued down into the valley. It looked like a still photograph of a raging river.

Another soldier dressed like the men at the lake greeted them and led the new arrivals over the bridge toward the castle.

"The others are all waiting in the Great Hall. We have to hurry."

Crossing the bridge, Tom noticed a fleet of snowmobiles and his pulse quickened. What had they gotten themselves into? They were in a tricky situation, to say the least: stuck on a remote glacier on the side of one of the highest mountains in the Alps, in midwinter, with no chance of backup. They were on their own.

"Let's hope this works out," Tom murmured as they passed through the huge door and entered the castle.

33

TABARKA, TUNISIA

A CONFUSING MIXTURE OF NOSTALGIA AND ANGER ROSE IN Cloutard when he stepped out of the taxi at the harbor in Tabarka. He had been there not so very long ago and yet it felt like an eternity, or if it had happened in another life. It was quiet at the harbor, as it always was in the evenings. Tabarka had stopped being a tourist destination years before, and now that winter had come there was even less going on. He looked out at the old fortress —built by the Lomellini family, an old Genoan merchant dynasty—that for years had been his retreat. His home.

Cloutard could not begin to estimate how much money he had put into rebuilding the old fortress and converting it into a palace—*his* palace. When he first laid eyes on the place it had been uninhabitable, and yet he had decided to settle there. For him and his business, it was the perfect location. In spite of its seclusion, all of the major excavation sites in Europe, Asia Minor and Africa were within easy reach. And it boasted large branching underground storerooms, secure as a dungeon. The police had never found a thing, apparently, though his storerooms had been practically bursting at the seams with artifacts and works of art. And up there on the highest level was the helipad, of course. His helicopter had finally saved his life. Or was it more Tom Wagner who'd pulled his head out of the noose?

His nostalgia gave way to fury as he strolled along the harbor and saw the wide path lined with torches that twisted around the peninsula to the fortress entrance. He had built all of it, and *SHE* had taken it all away. He recalled briefly how he had first got to know Ossana Ibori, and how impetuous, intense and passionate their love affair had been. He had trusted her blindly and she had set him up, stripping away the work of a lifetime in seconds. She had used his contacts, infiltrated his network and showered everyone on his payroll with money—or used other forms of leverage—to pull them over to AF's side. And from one moment to the next, perhaps the greatest art thief and smuggler the world had ever seen had become a penniless joke. And he had not yet found a way to take back his power and everything that went with it. But perhaps now the time was ripe. The don's offer to put him back at the helm with the help of the Italian families was tempting and held a lot of promise. With the Mafia united behind him, they would put Ossana and AF—and whoever was behind AF—in their place.

And now he'd come back to get something important. There had been no time for it back then: he and Tom had had to flee for their lives in his helicopter when his own guards, suddenly taking orders from his supposed lover Ossana, had turned their guns on him.

He had to break into his old office and retrieve the key and the magnetic card for his safe deposit box in Luxembourg. Fortunately, foresight had led him to have a secret passage constructed during the renovation work, a tunnel that would allow him to come and go unnoticed if it ever became necessary. No one knew about it, not even Ossana. And now he would use the passage for the first and probably only time—to break into his own fortress.

Cloutard turned left off the path to the entrance and circled the peninsula, on the end of which rose the fortress. The edifice had been built to prevent capture from the sea, its walls founded on high, sheer cliffs that dropped into the Mediterranean. Tom had once told him that, back then, he had considered trying to enter the fortress from that side but had rejected it as impossible.

Tom, of course, knew nothing of the secret passage Cloutard was about to use. He trudged along the beach on the western side of the peninsula until he came to an old, man-made stone jetty stretching far out into the sea. Out there, everything was already in complete darkness.

During the day, a few bathers would normally be swimming in the small lagoon. The sand was perfectly white, the water turquoise and crystal clear, and practically waveless; the lagoon was enclosed on three sides. Now there was not a soul in sight, and the sound of the ocean calmed Cloutard's nerves. How many times had he sat up on the terrace of his fortress and listened to that sound? Even now he remembered the last time he had been up there, with Tom and Ossana. And just a few short hours later, he had been sitting in his pajamas in an Italian prison, his life turned upside down.

Cloutard shook off the dark memories and walked up to the small ruin near the jetty. The ruin was no more than a few dilapidated pieces of wall a short way up the hill, visible from the jetty. No one had ever discovered the entrance he had created there, hidden by a few bricks, that led directly into the cellars beneath the fortress.

Minutes later, a flashlight lighting his way, Cloutard was ready to storm his own fortress. He opened another secret door and found himself in one of the storage rooms he had once used as intermediate storage for smuggled items. It was empty, just like all the other rooms through which Cloutard was now making his way. Ossana and AF had cleared everything out and, with the help of his old contacts, pushed it all onto the black market. It would have brought in tens of millions for AF —financing for their machinations all over the world. He had glimpsed their capabilities in the last year. He could only hope that the living quarters and especially his office were unchanged; otherwise, he had a problem. Standing in front of the steps leading up to the kitchen, a tired smile flashed across his face as he remembered how he had spent countless hours at the stove with his cook, a man he had brought in especially from Paris. He climbed the steps and realized immediately that the kitchen was unchanged. In fact, it was clearly still in use. There was fresh food in the refrigerator and a smell of recent cooking in the air.

Cloutard left the kitchen and stepped into the large reception hall. The beam of his flashlight moved over the old columns, crafted of marble that he had also had flown in especially. The bullet holes that had appeared in the course of his escape had been repaired, so someone was certainly taking care of his old home—and his anger returned at the thought of who it might be. He crept through the reception hall and peered up the wide staircase that led from the hall to the bedrooms on the second floor.

The house lay in silence and darkness. Quietly, he pushed open the door of his old office and tiptoed into the room. His office was where he had kept his most valuable relics, but they, too, had all disappeared. He pushed aside the empty desk as quietly as he could and flipped back the old Persian rug he'd stolen from Shah Reza Pahlavi's former palace in Tehran in the 1990s. Then he lifted a thin slab of stone to reveal a palm scanner and display hidden underneath.

He placed his palm on the scanner's glass plate, and it recognized him immediately. At least the safe had apparently remained undiscovered. The touch screen next to the scanner came to life and displayed a block of numbers. Cloutard smiled as he typed in the twelve-digit code and another stone slab, considerably larger and thicker, dropped a few inches with a soft hiss and slid to the side. He shone his flashlight into the floor safe and could see immediately that everything was still in place. Quickly, he found the leather folder that contained the state-of-the-art vault key and the magnetic card that went with it.

That was when the lights came on.

34

MATTERHORN GLACIER, SWITZERLAND

Two soldiers pushed the massive, creaking double doors open. Tom gulped. Was today the day he would finally discover his limits?

Someone had led Edward away already, and he had no idea where he'd been taken. The doc was right, Hellen would never forgive him if they didn't get out of there alive. Tom absorbed every little detail around him. An endless array of doors, stairs and corridors, a real labyrinth. He suspected that they would take Hellen's father to a dungeon somewhere below. Castles like this always had dungeons. He couldn't see any more guards— in fact, he had only counted five or six so far, not including the pair at the helicopter. Very few for such a big place, but then he recalled that he was in the middle of nowhere. The weather there was probably more dangerous than any imagined intruders. Still, he couldn't be sure. They might have an entire army tucked away in a cellar.

"Forgive my tardiness, my king," said Lancelot, pushing

past Tom into the immense hall. Tom could hardly contain his amazement, but he knew he couldn't let anything show. Twelve gigantic statues of knights were arranged in a circle around the hall, each one holding a sword stretched skyward. The tips of their swords met just beneath the top of the vaulted ceiling, a hundred feet overhead. A circular chandelier of forged steel, held in place by twelve chains attached to the free arms of the statues, hung over the table. Between the statues, small flames burned in twelve braziers. Opposite the entrance, between two statues, was a stained-glass window displaying a magnificent variation of the insignia of the ring Tom wore.

Lancelot scurried to his place at the table, snapped his heels together and saluted in the now-familiar fashion.

"Hail, Sir Lancelot," said the man to Lancelot's right. King Arthur himself. *Or more likely someone who thinks he's the descendant of King Arthur*, Tom speculated. The man was older and wore an elegant three-piece suit and a black mask, just like everyone else around the table. Tom had to hold back a smirk—something about the masks reminded him of Batman. *Why are these people always so damned theatrical?* he wondered.

Tom walked through the portal and headed straight for the gigantic stone table. There were still two seats free, and he would be in serious trouble if he chose the wrong one. The table was divided into twelve segments, like a clock, with twelve swords arranged in a star shape. Fortunately for Tom, a relief of each knight's shield had been carved into the heavy stone slabs. His place was exactly opposite Arthur's.

"You too, Sir Galahad. Welcome!"

Arthur, whoever he really was, spread his hands wide, and the men all took their seats at the same time. The slim, ornately carved backs of the chairs towered over their heads. There, too, their respective coat of arms had been worked into the wood. Now that he was sitting, Tom took a closer look at the swords. They were smaller than he would have expected, more like the weapon of a Roman centurion than the longswords used by medieval knights.

"I thank you all for responding to the call of your king. Today is a great day. We have come another step closer to our goal."

Arthur raised a small, rolled-up leather cover. Tom's pulse quickened. *It that really another part of the Chronicle? Can it be true? So close, but still out of reach.* So he not only had to get Edward out of there alive, he also had to get his hands on that part of the Chronicle— ideally unnoticed, and as quickly as possible. He didn't want to spend a second longer than necessary in here. Every passing moment increased the risk of being spotted.

"Our predecessors spent hundreds of years searching for this, but now the time has come. The Chronicle will be reunited and can finally reveal its secrets. Unfortunately, not all of our brave knights are able to share in this victory." Arthur's gaze turned to the empty chair. For a moment, an oppressive silence settled, and all of the men at the table lowered their heads. Tom could almost hear his own heartbeat. Then Arthur turned to each knight in turn and asked them to report. He called on them one after the other, in no particular order. Tom looked around the assembly, but his attention was less on the seated men and more on the architecture of the monumental hall. He needed a plan.

A shudder ran through him when he consciously registered the presence of the six-foot high braziers between each pair of statues. Fire blazed in each one, and Tom could not avoid thinking back to Barcelona and the flaming inferno that braziers very much like these had caused there. Fire was Tom's only weakness, a deep-seated phobia that went all the way back to the death of his parents. But that mission, almost a year ago now, had largely cured him of his fear. At least, he hoped it had.

Finally, Arthur called on Lancelot. "My dear Lancelot has managed to discover the location of the next section, haven't you?"

"Yes, my king." He rose to his feet. "We found a clue in Istanbul. A chamber has been discovered in the famous cisterns beneath Topkapi Palace. Some of the items that have been found have been transferred to the museum under tight security. They were moved before I had an opportunity to obtain them."

"Go on," Arthur said sternly. Lancelot grew nervous.

"I am sorry, my king, but there was nothing I could do by myself. The local authorities had reinforcements, and there were two Blue Shield agents on site as well. I was tipped off just in time to avoid arrest when I tried to examine the discoveries. And I was able to liquidate the two agents, but then I had to flee." Tom's eyes widened. *Two Blue Shield agents are dead? Thank God Hellen's in Glastonbury and not in Turkey.* Lancelot went on, "For the moment, the discovery is safe. I believe that neither the authorities nor Blue Shield has any idea what they've really found."

"Lancelot, you are not exactly living up to your reputation as my first knight. Put a team together and get us that piece as soon as possible. And don't let me down me again," Arthur said icily, putting Lancelot in his place. The man resumed his seat meekly.

So they're completely ruthless. They'll kill for what they want without a second thought. Good to know.

"And now we come to you, Sir Galahad," Arthur said, looking directly at Tom. "And I believe you've brought something along with you."

35

TABARKA, TUNISIA

CLOUTARD LOOKED UP INTO THE EYES OF OSSANA IBORI, dressed in hotpants and a t-shirt and aiming a SIG Sauer P320 at his head.

"You used to sleep naked, *mon chérie*, did you not?" Cloutard said. As deftly as a magician, he'd secreted the key and the magnetic card beneath his jacket. He'd spent a good part of his youth working the streets of Milan, Siena, Florence and Pisa as a pickpocket, and he still had quick fingers.

"Living here alone, I don't feel the need to play the *femme fatale* all the time," Ossana said calmly.

Cloutard had his hands raised now and was back on his feet.

"Thank you for showing me the safe. I had our people scour this place for months. Well done, François, you hid this one really well." She pointed at the hole in the floor. "We'll go through your papers now in our own time. But there's another thing, François . . ."—Ossana pointed the barrel of the pistol at the right side of Cloutard's jacket— ". . . I want whatever you just put in your pocket, too." She shifted the gun to his head again and held out her other hand. "*S'il vous plait*, Monsieur Cloutard," she said cynically, with the ugliest French accent Cloutard had ever heard.

He screwed up his face and reached into his jacket pocket.

"Gently, gently," Ossana said. "Two fingers, please." And she watched as Cloutard withdrew the shiny metal key from his pocket and, with a scowl, placed it in her hand.

Without warning, a shot rang out. Ossana's eyes opened wide, and her face twisted in pain. She grabbed at her shoulder.

"A pistol? But . . . I thought you hated weapons," she groaned.

A second later, Cloutard's fist crashed into her face. Her nose broke and she fell backwards, banging her head hard. She lay on the floor without moving. Cloutard quickly took back his key.

"I have been known to overcome my prejudices if the situation requires it," he murmured.

He slipped the North American Arms Pug, a small .22-caliber revolver, back into his jacket pocket. His pickpocketing days had paid off once again, and he was still a master of one of the most important skills—palming. He had hidden the mini-revolver in the palm of his hand as he passed the key to Ossana. He stepped over the woman lying on the floor, not looking back as he went down the stairs and left the fortress by the secret entrance. Fifteen minutes later, he was in a taxi heading for the airport.

36

INSTITUTE FOR FORENSIC STUDIES, UNIVERSITY OF ISTANBUL

VITTORIA ARCANO NEEDED SOME FRESH AIR. SHE'D SEEN dead bodies before, of course, but the sight of her two dead Blue Shield colleagues had affected her more than she thought it would. She had to report back to Theresia de Mey in Vienna and consult with her about the best way to proceed. But she stopped. If Theresia found out the two agents were dead, she would surely order Vittoria back to her desk. She would never hand over responsibility for a situation like this to Vittoria. But she was a trained investigator. She'd been on the verge of a career with Interpol, and Interpol didn't take just anyone. It was only because of the chance encounter with Tom at the train station in Rome that her career had gone in a different direction. She could do this.

She decided to make some independent inquiries of her own, updating Theresia only when she had something solid to go on. Maybe she would find something that would give her a strong argument to allow her to continue her investigation there. But what was her next move? She knew nobody locally, had no contacts, and couldn't access the infrastructure of either UNESCO or Blue Shield—to say nothing of Theresia's network.

"*Hanmefendi*, are you the woman from Blue Shield?"

Vittoria heard a squeaky voice behind her, and it took her a second to come out of her thoughts and realize that someone had just spoken to her. She turned and saw a short man wearing a simple kaftan and a friendly smile.

"Who wants to know?"

Vittoria was on the alert. She had just seen two dead colleagues. If she wasn't careful, she might be next.

The man bowed slightly. "I am Bayhan Erdemi, *hanıme-fendi*. I was the guide for your two UNESCO colleagues. I am inconsolable about your loss."

"Anyone could say that," Vittoria said stiffly.

Bayhan took out a few papers from beneath his kaftan.

"Here is the contract I had with them. Of course, I had to sign a confidentiality agreement. Here are the two signatures and the Blue Shield stamp."

Vittoria looked through the paperwork. They could have been stolen or forged, of course, but the little man seemed honest enough. Her gut feeling told her to give him a chance. She handed the papers back, looked at him intently, and waited. Bayhan understood.

"As you know, the subterranean cisterns are one of the biggest tourist attractions here in Istanbul. But a few days ago, they were closed, and all tours and visits have now been canceled indefinitely. The tour guides in Istanbul are furious. People are saying things about a sensational discovery in the cisterns, which would explain the closure and also why your colleagues were here."

Vittoria nodded and Bayhan went on. "I took your colleagues to the cistern and I organized it so that they could be present for all appraisals. After we delivered the first items to the Topkapi Palace, I did not hear from them again. The must have gone back down to the cisterns unescorted, because I only learned what happened to them when I read about it in the newspaper."

Vittoria sensed that there was more to come. Something was still weighing on Bayhan's heart, but for now she left it at that.

They had walked a short way while Bayhan was talking and had reached Vittoria's rental car. The Forensics Institute was out on the western edge of Istanbul. Vittoria had needed transport and she had no interest in haggling with taxi drivers about the price, only to get ripped off. She decided spontaneously to trust Bayhan.

"With my Blue Shield ID, I should at least be able to get some information out of the Topkapi Palace," she said, more to herself than to Bayhan. "Get in. You're my guide now. We're going to Topkapi Palace. Maybe we'll find out more there, perhaps even a clue about who killed my colleagues."

Forty-five minutes later, they reached the huge palace estate. Ten minutes after that they came out again, empty-handed. Vittoria was furious.

"I have never seen anyone treat an official UNESCO

representative like that. They treated me like dirt in there."

Vittoria was furious, and Bayhan laid his hand reassuringly on her shoulder. "If you like, I'll ask around a little," he said. "Perhaps there is a way to enter the cisterns that will open with a little baksheesh."

Bayhan had reached for his cell phone and was already deep in a loud conversation in Turkish. Then he hung up.

"This might take some time. I will try to find a way for us to get inside as quickly as I can. Until then, I would suggest you lay low. You never know who you can trust," Bayhan said.

"Including you?"

Bayhan laughed. "All I know is this: money rules the world, and it is no different in a country like mine. Go back to your hotel and let me do what I can."

Vittoria looked at Bayhan and her uncertainty returned. Should she take the risk? Should she go on digging on her own? In a way, she was almost glad that she didn't have to decide right away. Bayhan could put his feelers out; if anything at all seemed suspicious to her, she could always pull out. They said goodbye and Vittoria climbed into her car. Just before she drove off, Bayhan knocked on her side window: "Remember: trust no one."

37

MATTERHORN GLACIER, SWITZERLAND

TOM'S HEART SKIPPED A BEAT. IT WAS OVER. HE WAS DONE for. Slowly he rose to his feet and was about to speak when, behind him, the huge double doors swung open, and a soldier stepped into the hall. The man marched quickly around the table, saluted King Arthur and whispered something in his ear. Then he turned on his heel and Arthur, after a very long pause, turned to his knights.

"Gentlemen, there has been a new development. For the moment, that is all I can tell you. Return to your quarters. We shall continue our meeting later."

The men rose to their feet. "Long live King Arthur," they intoned in unison. Tom turned with the others to leave, but Arthur spoke again.

"Sir Galahad! A word, if you please." Tom stopped in his tracks.

The door closed with a thunderous crash behind the last knight to leave, the boom resounding unpleasantly through the hall and setting Tom's teeth on edge. Then silence fell. The two soldiers who had closed the doors were still in the room. Tom didn't dare to breathe. He turned around and looked directly at Arthur.

"How can I be of service, my king?" he asked, sounding unbearably stupid in his own ears. Arthur rose from his throne. At that moment, the two soldiers grabbed hold of Tom from behind.

"Hey! What is this?" Tom protested, although he'd reckoned with no less.

Arthur slowly circled the table and approached.

"It's actually very simple. I have just been informed that the body of Lord Whitlock has been found in Venice, and that the police are treating his death as murder. If that is the case, then I can only wonder who I have sitting in my dungeon. And if Lord Whitlock is no longer among the living, then it is safe to assume that my loyal knight Sir Galahad has failed in his task, and that you killed him."

Only a few paces separated the two men now. Arthur stopped and looked Tom up and down. With a nod, he ordered the soldiers to remove Tom's mask, and they did so.

"Thomas Maria Wagner, in the flesh." Arthur looked puzzled for a moment. "Is it pronounced 'Wagner' or more like 'Vahgner'? Your father was American, so one would tend to think 'Wagner.' On the other hand, you grew up in Vienna and still live there. And in Vienna, one would naturally say 'Vahgner,' like the famous composer. So which is it? Wagner or 'Vahgner'? One more thing. I don't mean to be impolite, but your English accent is quite abysmal."

"It's Wagner," Tom growled. Who the hell was this guy, and how did he know so much about him? He'd been thinking about who was behind the mask the whole time, but he was fairly sure he'd never met the man. But he could not be part of AF, that much was clear.

"All right. Wagner it is. Your reputation precedes you. You've caused quite a stir in the last year. And I must say, I'm a bit honored that you've paid me a visit."

The two soldiers held Tom in an iron grip and Tom's attempts to break free somehow were useless.

"This man," Arthur said, addressing the soldiers now but with an appreciative nod toward Tom, "is a true hero. Vienna, Barcelona, Russia, Ethiopia, and the United States. You certainly do get around. And in the end, there you always stand: the victor." Arthur actually applauded, turning back to Tom and looking him in the eye.

"You would be perfect knight material, you know. But I somehow doubt that I could convince you to work for me. Or could I? Two positions are open, as you know."

"Over my dead body," Tom said through gritted teeth.

Arthur shook his head. "Mr. Wagner, be careful what you wish for," he said, lifting an index finger in warning. "There's one thing you should know. Your success story ends here and now. Get him out of my sight. I'll take care of both of them later." With that, Arthur turned and went back to his throne, picked up the second piece of the Chronicle and left the hall through a hidden door behind one of the statues.

38

BRITISH ORTHODOX CHURCH
SECRETARIAT, CHARLTON, LONDON

MAX HAD METICULOUSLY OBSERVED THE SPEED LIMIT ON the motorway and streets from Glastonbury to London, and now he was driving the rental Vauxhall through London traffic with extreme discipline. Hellen could not believe that a man could so consistently bow to every rule, and briefly wondered how Max would behave during sex. Did he follow a set of rules for that, too? Did he have a list he could check off? A schedule? A little book of dos and don'ts? She shuddered at the thought and realized her tedium must have reached a new low if she was thinking about things like that.

She had gone over everything having to do with Father Montgomery a dozen times in her mind but had come up with nothing. What did the priest have to do with any of this? Was there really a connection between what that had happened a year earlier and their assignment now? Was it all a coincidence, or was AF pulling strings in the background, working on another of their perfidious, globe-spanning plans? The death of the two Blue Shield agents also threw up questions. She decided not to rack her brain any further. Perhaps their interview with the Seraphim of Glastonbury, the patriarch of the British Orthodox Church, would shed some light on things.

Max parked the car in front of the secretariat. When he got out, he checked that the car was perfectly parallel, at the correct distance from the curb. Then he went around and folded in the side mirrors. Hellen raised her eyebrows in annoyance. Having both Tom and Max in this team would never work. And from what Tom had told her, the two had never been a team in the past, either. Well, that was her mother's problem, not hers. It was Theresia who'd brought Max in, after all, so it was up to her to figure out how to handle elements as incompatible as fire and water in one unit.

Hellen and Max entered the secretariat.

"Hellen de Mey," Hellen said to the young priest at reception. "We're here in the name of UNESCO and would like to speak for a moment with the Seraphim about Father Montgomery's death last year."

The young priest's eyes widened for a moment, but he quickly regained his composure.

"I'll see if the Seraphim has time," he said, picking up the phone. He passed on Hellen's reason for coming in a few words, with particular emphasis on "Father Montgomery." Then he listened patiently for a moment before saying, "Yes, Eminence."

Then the young priest hung up. "I'm sorry, but the Seraphim is very busy right now and cannot see you. But you're welcome to make an appointment." He began leafing through a datebook. "Yes, here," he said. "I can squeeze you in three weeks from today. What time would suit you?"

"In three weeks?" Hellen did not varnish her displeasure at all. "Are you trying to—" Hellen interrupted herself. "Five minutes. He can't even find that? Not even five minutes in the next three weeks? We're from UNESCO!"

The priest went back through the datebook and shook his head. "I'm afraid not."

Hellen took a deep breath. She was raging inside and glared at Max, who made no move to do anything. Tom would probably have marched right past the protesting priest. Not Max. She couldn't expect any help from him at all.

Everything by the book, she thought. *Then we'll just have to come up with something else. And from what I've seen of these situations, he's not going to like my solution one bit.*

She turned on her heel, grabbed Max's sleeve, and stormed out of the secretariat. Max trotted tamely along behind. Hellen had immediately taken out her phone and opened Google Maps.

"Give me the keys. Charlton Cemetery is just a few minutes from here. I'll drive." She held out her hand and Max handed over the key without a word.

Hellen didn't notice that the same black car that had been following them since their arrival in England was still on their tail. It had followed them out to Glaston-bury and back to London. When they stopped at the cemetery a few minutes later, it rolled past innocently.

Hellen and Max were in time to see the large wrought-iron gates being closed. The cemetery attendant had stopped outside the entrance, climbed out of his car, and was closing the gates, which were flanked by the red-brick columns typical of English graveyards. Hellen jumped out of her car and marched over to the man.

"Excuse me, sir, but why are you already closing?"

The man looked at her peevishly and barked his answer in a broad cockney accent. Hellen struggled to make sense of his words.

"The Seraphim's just asked me t' take care o' somethin' important for 'im, Miss. Seein' as I'm alone 'ere, I've got no choice. Y' can come back tomorrow."

Hellen sighed. This was not her day. "One more question. Do you know where Father Montgomery's grave is?"

The man flinched visibly at the question. He hesitated, but then replied, "That's easy. Left past the Cemetery Chapel and all the way t' the back until the road turns t' the right. Then straight on until it makes another right. Then y' follow the rows o' graves back t' the trees, right on the cemetery wall. But y' can only come tomorrow. Sorry, Miss."

Just then, he heard a low rumble and looked up. A winter storm was brewing. The wind picked up and the first ice-cold drops of rain spattered the ground.

The man flipped up his collar, tipped a finger to his baseball cap, climbed into his car, and drove off. Hellen already had her phone in her hand and was following the man's directions on the map. Directly behind the cemetery wall was a patch of land that, according to Google, belonged to the Defence Support Group, a British government organization responsible for maintaining military equipment. A couple of taps opened the Street View function, where she could see an armed soldier posted at the entrance—so no way to jump the wall there.

"What are you doing, Hellen?" Max asked. He was looking over her shoulder as she ran through her options for getting into the cemetery. The rain was getting heavier, and they got back into the car.

"I'm looking for a way for us to get in there now. What do you think I'm doing?"

"But the cemetery's closed. That would be trespassing or disturbing the peace or something. It would be illegal."

Hellen had been expecting that. But one thing was clear to her. However all this turned out and whether or not Tom would be back on the team, Max was out. Gone. Fired. Big time.

"Max, we don't have time to sit around. People are getting killed, as you saw for yourself in Venice." She looked around. "There are criminals out there also searching for the Chronicle of the Round Table, they will stop for nothing and nobody, and they do not play by your rules."

As she spoke, she realized that since they had arrived in England, she had never once considered that they might be in danger themselves, and the realization annoyed her immensely. Tom would have thought of it.

"So we have to stay on this." She pointed at her display. "On the northwest side there's a residential area that borders the cemetery grounds. Trees cross the walls from the other side. I think we can probably climb over the wall there without being seen." She paused for a second and glared at Max. "And you know what? We actually hired you because this kind of thing is your job. I'm not here to make plans and figure out how to break into things. And for God's sake, forget the fucking rules and regulations, please! You're not in the police anymore. Imagine you're in a war!"

Max's expression changed. Her words had obviously hit home. He took Hellen's iPhone. He expanded and compressed the map and checked the cemetery surroundings.

"Main Street here, DSG premises here, residential here, Queen Elizabeth hospital here," he murmured.

He zoomed in on every possible access point around the cemetery and nodded. "You're right. This is our best chance."

He climbed out of the car, went around to the trunk and took out his pistol, which they had brought along in their diplomatic baggage as UNESCO employees. The rain was pouring down now. They ran along Cemetery Lane to the north and turned right at the end of the cemetery wall, where a row of two-story houses stood.

Two sets of eyes watched their every move. And when Hellen and Max turned the corner, two men climbed out of the black car and followed them, staying well back.

39

MATTERHORN GLACIER, SWITZERLAND

THE TWO SOLDIERS MANHANDLED THEIR STRUGGLING prisoner down the tight spiral staircase. At the bottom, they turned into a long passageway. Electrical cables were strung from one torch mounting to another. The brackets had been retrofitted for electricity and each one held a weak light bulb that gave off no more than a gleam.

The deeper they pushed into the castle, the colder it became, and Tom soon saw ice crystals on the walls. When they passed through another heavy wooden door with iron fittings, they reached the middle of the dungeon: a low-ceilinged octagonal room that, like the passage, was lit by weak light bulbs. In the dim light, Tom could make out seven cells with low vaulted ceilings, most of them apparently for storage, filled with large wooden crates and modern flight cases. Only one cell looked empty. One of the soldiers let go of Tom and went straight to the cell, unlocked the rusted but solid door and stepped inside. In a recess on the opposite wall stood a field cot, and on the cot, curled up, lay a blanket-covered figure.

Doc, this is really not the time for a nap, even if it's colder than the ninth circle of hell, Tom thought as the second soldier led him into the cell. He was looking feverishly for the right moment to try to take the two soldiers down.

"Hey! Move your ass, you've got company," the soldier snarled, and he turned the body on the bed over. An unconscious man rolled off the cot, and to the surprise of everyone, it wasn't Edward de Mey.

"What the hell?" exclaimed the soldier, who jumped back when he recognized the face of one of his fellow guards.

I'm impressed, Doc, Tom thought with a smile. He was pleasantly surprised to discover that he'd probably underestimated Hellen's father. The aging archaeologist had vanished. The soldier spun around and froze. Tom could see his wide-open eyes even through his protective goggles. He was staring down the barrel of the Heckler & Koch pistol in the shaking hand of the second soldier.

"Drop the gun," the second soldier ordered, with a slight tremble in his determined voice, but still with determination.

"Edward?" Tom was thrilled to realize.

"Don't just stand there, disarm the man," Edward said with considerably more confidence now.

Still surprised at this sudden serendipitous turn of events, Tom relieved the first soldier of his rifle and sidearm.

"Undress!" Edward ordered. He seemed to be taking genuine pleasure in his newfound power.

The man reluctantly complied and stripped off his combat gear, helmet and mask. Delighted, Tom stripped down as well and slipped into his new disguise, as usual adapting quickly to the sudden change in his fortunes.

"Okay, now for the uncomfortable part. On your knees." Tom took the sidearm and pressed it to the man's forehead as he knelt, shivering. "Where does Arthur keep it?"

"You'll never make it out of here. You're as good as dead, both of you," the man spat.

Tom smashed the butt of the pistol into the man's nose, and blood streamed down his face. When he was kneeling straight again, Tom demonstratively cocked the hammer of the gun in front of the man's face and pressed it hard into his temple.

"I'm only going to ask twice."

"Tom!" Edward shouted in shock.

"East tower, second floor. In his room," the soldier snuffled, his face screwed up in pain.

"See? That wasn't so hard. Thanks a lot."

Edward shook his head, appalled at what he'd just witnessed. Tom took the assault rifle and bashed the soldier on the head with the butt, sending him to dreamland. He slung the rifle over his shoulder.

"What was that all about?" Edward asked.

"Well, at least he's not shivering anymore," Tom joked.

He pushed Edward ahead of him out of the cell, slammed the door and locked it.

"I meant—"

"I know what you meant. And we still have a little job to take care of before we get out of here," Tom said.

"What? What did you find out?"

"You'll never believe me," Tom said, and in few words brought Edward up to date.

"Part of the Chronicle? Here?"

"You got it. We just have to steal it from that Arthur groupie and then figure out how the hell we're going to get away from this place. Give me a hand. Maybe we'll find something down here to help us."

The two men set to work searching through the countless flight cases and crates.

"Wow! These guys are serious," Tom said when he stumbled onto a crate of C4. "Are they trying to start a war?" He stuffed a few blocks of the stuff into a backpack, along with a handful of timer fuses. He pressed one of the fuses into a block of C4 on the spot and armed it.

"What do you think?" asked Edward after he'd opened one of the crates with a prybar. Bedded in straw were several anti-tank rocket launchers, and Edward, grinning broadly, held one up for Tom to see.

Tom let out a quick laugh. "I think if we run around here with one of those, we'll draw just a tad too much attention," he said, and Edward, a little disappointed, replaced the tank destroyer in its crate.

"Pack a few of those magazines, then we'll have everything we need. We can create all the diversions we need with the C4."

Tom took his pistol and carefully opened the door, then they slipped quickly along the passageway and back upstairs.

"How did you manage to get out of your cell?"

"I didn't let them lock me in in the first place. Thank you, by the way. This was very useful." Edward handed Tom a knife. "I found that in the back of your car," he added, when he saw the surprise on Tom's face.

"No, keep it. You never know."

"How many soldiers are running around here, anyway? Best guess?"

"We've taken care of two, and I counted five on the way in, but that doesn't mean much. You?"

"I saw two in the entrance area, and I think two in the courtyard. But we can't forget the Knights of the Round Table."

"No, we can't. But some of them were older men. They won't all be dangerous, but we need to be careful."

Tom cautiously opened a door very slightly and peered through the gap into the great vestibule of the Great Hall. Enormous staircases led upwards on the left and right of the gigantic double doors. Two men were standing guard at the portal that led back outside.

"But first we'll need a plan."

40

CHARLTON CEMETERY, LONDON, ENGLAND

It only took them a few minutes after climbing the wall to find the way the man at the gate had described. Apparently, he had been forced to leave in a rush: as Hellen and Max headed toward the chapel, they passed his small flatbed truck, the back piled high with gardening tools and cuttings. The wind was turning into a gale, and branches and foliage were flying from the truck bed and scattering across the cemetery. The rain stung as it whipped their faces, but they soon reached the fork leading to Father Montgomery's grave.

"What exactly are we doing here?" Max asked. He'd been asking himself the question ever since they'd climbed over the wall but hadn't found the courage to put it to Hellen before now.

But Hellen was clueless. She stared doggedly ahead as she marched through the ice-cold wind and rain, her lips pressed together tightly. The weather wasn't helping her mood, but she also had no answer to Max's question. So she said nothing. *And where's Tom when we need him? He would have had a plan in place hours ago.* Everything they were doing was ridiculous. She really had no idea what she was looking for.

"Here's the grave," Hellen shouted over the wind, pointing to a plain headstone on a patch of lawn.

The headstone was engraved with no more than the priest's name and two dates. Max hurried over.

"You know what I've been wondering all this time?" Hellen asked rhetorically. "Since the Seraphim's office brushed us off so rudely? Why in the world were Father Montgomery's body and his possessions moved all the way from Glastonbury to here, only to be buried in a simple grave like this? I'm fairly sure that he was born and raised in Glastonbury, so it would make more sense if were buried there with his family, right?"

Max shrugged indifferently and looked around.

What would you do now, Mr. Wagner? Hellen wondered. And the first thing that came to her was so crazy it could have come straight from Tom.

"Let's open the grave," she said.

"You want to . . . what?" Max was hoping he'd misheard, but he soon found out there was nothing wrong with his ears.

"Run back to that truck and grab a couple of shovels. We have to hurry. The light is already starting to go."

Max tried to protest, but Hellen's glare told him it wouldn't make any difference. If he didn't help her, she'd dig the priest up by herself. If there was one thing he'd learned in the short time he'd been around her, it was that resistance was useless. Together, it would go much faster, so off he went.

The two men who'd been tailing them were able to duck behind a stand of birches when they saw Max coming. He climbed up onto the flatbed, now practically empty of branches and foliage, and grabbed a spade, a shovel and a crowbar. When he got back to the grave, he went to work with the shovel. Hellen grabbed the spade and started digging beside him.

The winter storm was in full swing, now. The frigid rain was falling on them in buckets as they worked to loosen the cold earth.

It was dark by the time they reached the coffin. They had jammed two flashlights into the earthen walls of the grave to give themselves at least a little light to work by. Soaked to the skin, they threw the shovels up out of the grave. On her knees, Hellen pushed the last layer of mud aside with her bare hands, freeing up the coffin lid, which was in two sections. The adrenaline in her system was making it hard to breathe. Desecrating a grave went far beyond a misdemeanor, but it had to be done.

"I expect you want me to open it, right?"

"You catch on quickly."

The lid of the coffin sprang open almost immediately when Max went to work on it with the crowbar.

"We're going to hell for this, you know," Max complained. "And when your mother finds out about it, I'll be out of a job again." He was clearly struggling with the situation.

"The whole lid," was all Hellen said.

She took one of the flashlights and shone the light into the coffin. Lying on white satin was the emaciated body of the old man. Max crossed himself.

"He's wearing one of those rings, too," Max said, pointing to the dead man's bony hand. On his ring finger he wore the same piece of jewelry that the assassin in Venice had been wearing. Hellen was sure, now. She hadn't just been imagining it. But what did a priest from Glastonbury have in common with a nameless killer? *Was he one of them? Was Father Montgomery a member of the Society of Avalon?*

"Is that it? Can we go now?" Max's impatience was growing. He didn't know much about English law, but he was pretty certain that doing what they were doing could have serious consequences. Without waiting for an answer from Hellen, he climbed out of the hole.

"Just one more thing," Hellen murmured. She put her feet on either side of the head part of the coffin and swung the lower half closed again. "If I remember correctly, coffins like this usually have a small drawer in the lid for holding burial objects." And there it was. She eased the small drawer out of the lid. Inside it was an old book, tied shut with a length of string. She slipped that inside her jacket, too, to keep it safe from the rain. Then she closed the lid again.

"Come on, help me up!" she called to Max, and he grabbed her hand and pulled her back to the surface.

"Thanks for doing the dirty work for us."

Max's hand instinctively flew to his gun. A shot rang out, and his head practically exploded.

"Max! NOOOO!" Hellen cried in panic as Max's body tumbled backward into the grave he'd just excavated and crashed onto the lid of the coffin.

Frozen, Hellen could only stare at the faces of the two men.

The one holding the Uzi nodded with satisfaction. "A man who knows his place," he said drily in his Welsh accent.

Hellen's tears mixed with the rain that ran frigidly over her face. Her whole body was shaking. Was this the end for her? She could think of only one thing. Tom.

Suddenly, a flash of lightning blazed and all three of them flinched. The bolt must have struck very close, because the thunder was instant and deafening. The two men spun around, looking for where the lightning had struck. This was her chance. Hellen made the most of their moment of distraction and ran.

41

MATTERHORN GLACIER, SWITZERLAND

Twenty minutes later, Tom and Edward put their plan into action. The explosives were in place and their escape prepared. Dressed as they were, they were able to move about the castle unchallenged, which made things much easier. There was only one moment when they were nearly exposed, but Tom was able to overpower a guard and hide his unconscious body behind a suit of armor. There really did seem to be very few soldiers guarding the place, and they were able to listen in to the radio traffic and plan accordingly. But the tricky part was coming now. They had to steal the second part of the Chronicle, which most likely meant another confrontation with the would-be king. They went up the eastern stairs, as the soldier had told them, turned a corner, and found themselves at a door.

"This must be it," said Edward. "In a castle like this, it's where the master's chambers would be."

Tom pressed his ear to the door. Nothing. The room seemed to be unoccupied. Cautiously and very slowly,

Tom lifted the bolt and pulled on the door. It was locked.

"What now? We don't have much time before the first charges goes up," Edward said, looking around nervously.

Tom checked his watch. "We improvise." He took the last block of C4 out of his backpack, carved off a small chunk of the plastic explosive, pressed it around the detonator, and pushed the mass into the ancient iron lock. He hesitated.

"We should wait a little. The first charges go off in ten minutes. If we blow this now, it'll be too early."

Edward swallowed, but finally nodded. A few minutes passed, and just as Tom was about to trigger the detonator the radio crackled, and an excited voice came through.

Tom listened, then said, "Shit! They know we're not where they put us. They're on their way. Cover me." Edward went back to the corner to watch the stairs. Tom triggered the detonator and ran to join him. Three seconds later, the small charge exploded. At the same moment, the first soldier came storming up the stairs. But Edward hesitated. Tom pulled him back around the corner, grabbed the rifle, and fired down at the charging soldiers.

"Go and find the Chronicle. I'll hold them off."

Edward did as he was told and disappeared into Arthur's room.

Suddenly, Tom heard a noise behind him. He turned and fired, hitting the man who'd just appeared around the opposite corner, but the soldier had been able to squeeze of a shot, too, and the bullet grazed Tom's arm.

"Fuck!" Tom snarled, his face screwed up in pain. "How's it going in there?" Tom shouted to Edward. Then he had an idea. He cut the rest of the C4 into two halves, pressed a detonator into each half, and placed the charges on opposite corners of the hallway. *Ten seconds ought to be enough*, he thought. At the last moment, he leaped into the room with Edward.

"Get down!" he screamed, hitting the floor hard as the two charges detonated.

"What have you done?" Edward shouted. "Now we're sitting in a trap!" He was starting to panic.

"You're right, we can't get out. But they can't get in, either. Quick, help me," Tom said calmly. The hotter things got, the cooler he became. Together, they barricaded the door with a chest of drawers.

"Better safe than sorry."

"You're hurt," Edward said.

"Just a flesh wound."

"Thank God for that, but at least we've got the Chronicle." Edward held the leather cover up triumphantly while Tom ran to the window to scout their only exit.

"Put it in there," Tom said, tossing the empty backpack to Edward, "and protect it with your life." He looked out the window. "The snowmobiles are just below us, but it's a long way down. I hope you're not afraid of heights."

Tom tore the curtains from their rod, took out his knife, nicked the fabric and tore it into strips.

"We're going to need at least five lengths." Tom threw his knife to Edward and began tying the ten-foot-long sections of cloth together while Edward got the next length ready. A glance at his watch told Tom that they only had four minutes before the first of their main charges blew.

Between them, they had their rough-and-ready rope finished in short order. Tom tied it to the curtain rod he'd pulled down and wedged the rod against the window frame.

"Okay. We're sliding down the small roof, then rappelling down from there. Understood?" Edward was white as a sheet, but he nodded. Just then, someone threw themselves against the door, making Edward jump.

"You first." Tom held their makeshift rope out to Edward. "Go!" he barked, looking between Edward and the door. The barricade was holding. For now.

Edward was climbing through the window when Tom's phone suddenly rang. Ossana.

"Not a good time, Ossana. I'm a little busy right now." Bam! Bam! The soldier outside kept hurling himself at the door.

"I hope you have good news for me soon. Remember, the vaccine for Hellen's father has a use-by date. If you don't deliver, he dies."

"Thank you. Very motivating." Tom hung up and looked down. Edward had only just reached the small roof. *Is his illness already making him weak?* Tom wondered.

Bam! Bam! The chest of drawers was starting to slip. Tom drew his gun and climbed onto the windowsill. Suddenly, the door flew open. Tom fired and dropped in the same moment. As he disappeared below the window, he saw the soldier hit the floor.

Holding the makeshift rope, Edward slid down the slope of the roof and had disappeared over the edge by the time Tom got there. With the gun in one hand and lowering himself with the other, Tom hit the roof harder than he had planned. He slipped, sliding out of control on the steep grade. He let go of the gun and only just managed to get both hands on the strip of curtain as he shot over the edge. He took a deep, relieved breath and shimmied down the last section to the ground.

"That was close," he said to Edward with a smile, but then instantly whipped him around and pulled him down as a soldier came running around the corner to the snowmobiles, firing as he ran. Tom returned fire with Edward's pistol, still in its holster, as they dropped, shooting the soldier down.

"Now I understand my daughter. You're completely crazy."

"Maybe. But you're still alive, aren't you? And we have the Chronicle."

Tom helped Edward to his feet, clapped him on the shoulder, and they swung together onto a snowmobile. Edward, sitting behind, held tightly to Tom as he opened the throttle wide. A high rooster tail of snow shot from the back as the machine sped away.

The first explosion boomed through the glacier valley, followed by a rumbling that didn't stop but seemed to be getting closer. Edward glanced back and saw two more soldiers jump onto their snowmobiles and take up the chase.

The avalanche triggered by the first explosion crashed down like a stormy sea onto the castle behind them. Tom stole a glance at his watch and grinned. *Perfect timing.* They were just rattling across the stone bridge, which shook both of them to the bone. Their pursuers were close behind, but they only made it to the middle of the bridge. Another explosion tore the bridge to pieces. The snowmobiles were hurled through the air and smashed onto the glacier below.

A sickle-shaped fan of snow flew as Tom's and Edward's snowmobile slewed to the right, sweeping past the parked helicopter, which was destroyed a moment later beneath a crushing rain of rocks.

After a few hundred yards, Tom stopped and looked back, admiring his handiwork.

"You can let go. We've made it," he said, and Edward finally loosened his grip. He turned and looked back up at the castle, too.

"Is this what you call archaeology at Blue Shield?"

"You tell me. You're the archaeologist. My job is to look after you. Now let's hope this thing has enough fuel to get us down to the valley," Tom said, roaring away again.

42

CHARLTON CEMETERY, LONDON, ENGLAND

HELLEN HAD MANAGED TO PUT AT LEAST A LITTLE DISTANCE between her and the men chasing her. Directly beside the row of graves was a stand of trees that also bordered the graveyard wall. She made it that far before she heard the Uzi firing and the first shots slamming into the trees and wall. The torrential rain had now turned to hail, and the world around her was going crazy, lightning, thunder, wind, and tiny pellets of ice whipping her in the face. She took note of it all only vaguely. All she had in her mind was survival. Her flight instinct—the same instinct that had saved the Neanderthals from the saber-toothed tiger and had survived in the human brain to the present day —had been awakened.

Run!

Find all the strength you can and keep running until you're safe.

Hellen made it to the cemetery wall, jumped, and pulled herself up. Normally even a single chin-up was beyond her, but now—with adrenaline coursing through her blood and facing the naked fear of death—she was over the wall in seconds. She knew perfectly well that the two men would execute her as callously as they had Max. They would not hesitate or stop to discuss the matter. But did they want the ring or the book? Whatever it was they were after, as soon as they had it, she was dead.

She swung her legs up and momentarily lay flat on top of the wall, and a bullet whistled past her head. In the wind, rain and lightning, she could not tell exactly where it had come from or how close the man was, but her gut told her: too damn close!

Run! Run!

She fell to the ground on the other side of the wall but was on her feet in a flash. She looked around. In front of her was a fence, behind which stood a large, opulent-looking house, almost too luxurious to have been built beside a cemetery. Another flash of lightning, another clap of thunder, and more hail. At first, the hail had been the size of rice grains, but now the falling stones were as big as walnuts. She pulled her hood tight with its two dangling cords, not wanting it to slide off the back of her head. A well-placed hailstone that big could knock her out. The house was dark, so it probably was not a good place to try to take refuge.

She heard the men scrabbling and saw the first of them appear on top of the wall. She turned to the right and ran toward the main street, deserted now because of the storm. A glance to the right: open land, no protection at all. A glance to the left revealed the same. No cover. In front of her was another stand of trees, and she thought she might have seen cars on the far side.

She ran on, heard more shots.

She crossed the street and had almost reached the cover of the trees when a burning pain lanced through her left shoulder. She stumbled and fell. The pain was indescribable but her body reacted instantly, producing even more adrenaline. Her face a mask of pain, she fought her way back to her feet and ran on. After a curve, she saw a small parking lot with about twenty cars parked in it. Behind the lot was a large white building that made her think "hospital." A gust of wind slammed into her from the right, almost knocking her off her feet, but the hood of one of the parked cars broke her fall. More pain racked her body, and she pressed a hand to her side. *Are my ribs broken now, too?* She thought. Ducking forward, her face twisted in pain, she looked for cover among the cars.

Go. Run. Survive.

At the end of the parking lot, she reached the back of the building. Her mind flashed back to what she'd seen on Google Maps when she was checking the area around the cemetery. She was at the back of the Queen Elizabeth Hospital.

More shots crashed into the wall beside her. She raced on.

Get to the entrance, she thought.

As she rounded the corner, she saw the main entrance ahead of her, and beyond it another parking lot. More parked cars, but still no one in sight. *No surprise there, not in weather like this*, she thought. The noise around her was becoming unbearable. Lightning, thunder, screaming wind, millions of hailstones crashing onto the asphalt and steel.

She ran for the main entrance. That would save her.

No cover at all.

Just a few more yards.

Hellen didn't hear the next shot. A searing pain sliced into her back, and her body pitched forward with the force of the bullet.

She opened her mouth in a mute scream.

Breathlessness.

One last step.

Hellen collapsed beneath the awning of the main entrance of Queen Elizabeth Hospital. Her vision clouded. Darkness.

43

KIRCHBERG PLATEAU, BANKING QUARTER OF LUXEMBOURG

Enormous palaces of steel, concrete and glass stood shoulder to shoulder. Only a few of the historical bank buildings had survived, which for François Cloutard was cause for regret. But you didn't always get to choose, and he'd been forced to store the holiest of his treasures in an ugly, modern fortress of a bank. Cloutard stepped into the expansive lobby, more reminiscent of a luxury hotel than a bank, and approached the reception desk.

He pushed his passport and the keycard across the counter to the man. "François Philibert Cyrille Cloutard."

The bank employee drew the magnetic card through a reader and checked Cloutard's passport. "Do you have your key?" he asked.

Cloutard handed him the key as well, and the man compared the serial number with the one in his system.

"The password, Monsieur," he said to Cloutard, indicating the terminal built into the counter.

"*Les Confidences d'Arsène Lupin*," Cloutard typed with pride into the touchscreen.

"Thank you, sir." The man nodded and reached for his telephone.

Two minutes later, a second employee approached.

"Monsieur Medeiros will accompany you downstairs," said the man behind the counter, and returned to his work. Cloutard and Medeiros looked one another in the eye, and it would have taken a very attentive observer to notice the almost imperceptible nod that passed between them.

The entered an elevator and rode seven floors below ground in silence. The elevator opened and Cloutard followed Medeiros through multiple checkpoints secured by voice recognition, magnetic keys, and numerical codes.

Once they had run the security gauntlet, they entered a room almost three hundred feet long, lined on both sides by seven-foot-high vault doors. Cloutard went to number 1138 and inserted his key in the keyhole. Medeiros took another key from a box inscribed with the logo "*Banque Privée Secrets Précieux*" and slipped it into a keyhole on the other side of the safe door. They turned their keys simultaneously, and the first of three small green lamps lit up. Then they pushed their magnetic cards into the appropriate slots beside the locks. The second green lamp glowed. Finally, Cloutard typed in a numerical code on his side. The third lamp illuminated, followed by an audible signal that played the beginning of the "Marseillaise."

The massive door swung open with a hiss. Medeiros nodded to Cloutard and left the room. When the almost 18-inch-thick door swung as wide as it would go, Cloutard stepped inside the vault. A normal vault like this would have been lit by the glare of neon lights, but this one was doused in a mystical beige by dimly glowing LEDs. Cloutard sighed as his eyes roamed over his treasures. It had been too long since he'd seen them. Here were Rembrandt's "The Storm on the Sea of Galilee" and Vermeer's "The Concert," both part of the haul from one of the most famous art thefts of the 20th century. Cloutard recalled happily the day in 1990 when they raided the Isabella Stewart Gardner Museum in Boston. It had been a tour de force. Beside the Vermeer leaned "Waterloo" by Claude Monet. On a small shelf stood Cellini's golden "Saliera," or salt cellar, purloined from the Museum of Art History in Vienna, and the "Borghorster Stiftskreuz," an Ottonian cross dating from the 11th century. Both objects had been later recovered by the police—except, of course, that that wasn't exactly true. Duplicates had been made to keep the embarrassment for the museums and local security services to a minimum. Not even Cloutard could estimate how many forgeries and counterfeits being passed off as originals were on display in the great museums of the world. Cloutard soaked up the ambience of the artworks for a few minutes before he turned to a leather case that also lay on the shelf. He opened it. Inside, in neat piles, lay bundles of 100-dollar bills.

"*Le pécule*," he murmured. His nest egg. He closed the case again, took a final look at his little collection, and exited the vault. With his keycard and key, he locked it again, then pressed a buzzer. Seconds later, Medeiros reappeared and checked everything. Moments later, they were both back in the high-speed elevator.

When Cloutard stepped out at ground level, the two men turned to face each other.

"The usual place?" Cloutard asked.

Medeiros nodded. "In one hour," he replied.

Sixty minutes later, Cloutard entered the Ladurée Luxembourg, a high-end café in Rue des Capucins in the center of the city. The place was as full as usual, with tourists ordering overpriced but sinfully delicious macaroons and cakes. In the rear section of the café, the *repas de midi*, the set lunch, was being served. Cloutard turned to the right and went up the carpeted stairs to the upper level. In a corner alone sat Fábio Medeiros. He stood up when Cloutard appeared and took a few steps toward him.

"*Velho amigo*," he greeted him quietly as they embraced. The two men went back a long way, not only as friends, but as business partners. Medeiros, originally from Portugal, had been Cloutard's accomplice for the Boston robbery.

Cloutard wasted no time. "I have hired Thorvald Brix for a new project."

Medeiros raised his eyebrows. "Is he still working?"

"Very much so. He may be old, but he is the best."

Medeiros was professional enough not to ask about the project.

"If his work is as good as it used to be, we should finally do what we've talked about, ever since Boston," said Cloutard.

"You want to have him forge the Vermeer and the Rembrandt?"

Cloutard nodded. "There are a few robberies I would still like to do, and after that I will retire. I have made a few new contacts who could be very helpful."

Medeiros nodded. "I have heard about your UNESCO work. I almost choked on my croissant when Adalgisa told me about it at breakfast. 'Francois is working for the good guys,' she said . . . not without a little mockery."

Cloutard did not want to probe any deeper into the "mockery" part. Instead, he said, "And how is your wife?"

"Bored to death. She hates my job, and she hates the fact that she has been sidelined. She keeps saying that she wants to go back to the front. Every day, all I hear is Boston, Boston, Boston, that we absolutely have to pull off another job like that."

Cloutard sipped at the *café au lait* that the waiter had brought as a matter of course and silently set down beside him.

"Give her my best. Maybe I can make her wish come true soon."

44

DECEMBER 1988, LAKE LLYDAW, SNOWDONIA, WALES

THE SNOWDON MASSIF IS ONE OF THREE MOUNTAIN groups in north Wales, occupying the area bounded by Pen-y-Pass and the villages of Beddgelert and Llanberis. The massif is surrounded by the peaks of Glyderau in the northeast, Moel Siabod in the east, Melwynion in the south, Moel Hebog, the Nantlle Ridge and Mynydd Mawr in the west. To the northwest, flatter land leads to Caernarfon and the Menai Strait. The rocks that form Snowdon are volcanic, dating to the Ordovician period, and the massif was heavily shaped by glacial action, creating the pyramid-shaped summits of Snowdon itself and the sharp ridges of Crib Goch and Y Lliwedd. The rock walls of Snowdon, including the face at Clogwyn Du'r Arddu, were used by Edmund Hillary to train for his ascent of Everest in 1953. The summit can be reached by various paths, and by the Snowdon Mountain Railway, a cogwheel rail line that opened in 1896 and carries passengers from Llanberis to the summit station.

Two men marched through the icy desert. The snow had begun to fall in early November this year and had continued for three weeks. The two men had bribed an employee of the cogwheel railway, allowing them to reach the mountain station relatively easily in the unfavorable weather. Otherwise, the expedition would have taken days. Both were young and in peak physical condition, but money was no particular object, so they had decided to take the easier route.

The men wore identical thick winter jackets with fur-lined hoods. The had snow boots and large backpacks for their equipment. At first glance, they looked very similar, but one of them wore a full beard.

"We'll have our hands full searching all of the possible locations," said Beard.

The other man nodded. "But we are lucky that everyone else is focusing on England and ignoring the importance of Wales."

"Which is incomprehensible to me. I mean, how can you just ignore the indications? Arthur's Stone in Gower, Maen Huail in Ruthin, Caerleon in Newport, Llyn Barfog, near Aberdyfi, Carreg Carn March Arthur, Dinas Emrys. The list goes on and on. Every single one of those places has a direct link to King Arthur."

The two men had reached the top of a rise. The white expanse was broken by two conspicuous patches— both white as well, but recognizable as frozen lakes.

Beard pointed down at one of them. "Allow me to present: Excalibur Lake!"

The other man clapped Beard on the shoulder. "We're in the right place. Those amateurs have always looked for the sword in the lakes, but of course they never found anything. They don't have our sources."

Beard put down his backpack and took out a photograph and a sextant. The photograph showed an ancient document, and he quickly scanned through the lines of text. Then he set to work with the sextant. The old-fashioned navigation instrument was used to measure the angular distance between two visible objects—usually between an astronomical object and the horizon when navigating by the stars, but it could also be used to work out a position between different mountain peaks. The principle of the instrument was first put to practical use by John Hadley in 1731 but was also found in the unpublished writings of Sir Isaac Newton.

"Just a few hundred yards more. That way." Beard pointed to the northwest, and the two men marched off. When they arrived at their destination, it was obvious. The crust of snow on sections of the slope was partially collapsed. The two men quickly cleared away the rest.

"An entrance!" Beard said excitedly.

"Good thing we came in winter. The weight of the snow's pressed the bushes down and made the entrance visible. it would all be overgrown in summer, and you wouldn't see it at all."

They worked for another ten minutes until they had completely cleared the snow from the entrance to a cave. Two flashlights snapped to life, and they began their descent, but after a few steps they realized that the cave floor was covered with a layer of ice and they stopped to put on crampons. They moved on cautiously through the tight, icy passages. The air was fresh, and although the cave floor was slippery and uneven, they made good progress. After a quarter of an hour, the passage widened and both men suddenly gasped.

Their flashlights roamed the cave they had stepped into —in reality more of a hall than a cave. The rough natural walls had abruptly disappeared, giving way to smooth masonry. Thrilled at their discovery, the two men took off their backpacks.

The hall was more than thirty feet high, and the ceiling was supported by twelve columns arranged in a circle. In a ring inside the circle of pillars were twelve small circles. The two men hurried to this inner ring and examined the floor. Then they looked at each other, knowing what they had found.

"Nineteen eighty-eight will go down in history. This is a breakthrough. These are the insignia of the Knights of the Round Table," Beard said, and his companion, grinning broadly, nodded.

In the minutes that followed, they explored the cavernous space. At one end, they found a huge stone with a large slot in it. Beard trembled as he pointed to it. Neither knew whether to feel thrilled or disappointed. They were standing in front of the stone that had once held Excalibur. But the sword wasn't there.

"Damn," Beard muttered.

"Not so fast," his colleague said. "See these fine

rectangular markings down here?" He was on his knees, working with a pocketknife at a small gap in the surface of the stone. Without warning, the two men heard a rumble and turned around in surprise. Something had moved on the floor, inside the circle of pillars. They ran back quickly and saw that the floor beneath Arthur's coat of arms had opened up. In the small space now exposed lay a wooden casket. The lifted it out carefully and lifted the lid to inspect the contents, but Beard's flashlight suddenly began to flicker.

"Battery's dead. I'll get fresh ones from the pack."

He stood up and went back to the entrance where they had left their backpacks. The other man continued to examine the casket.

"Oh my God!" he shouted. "You won't believe what's in here. We've done it! We've found part of the Chronicle of the Round Table!"

But those were his final words. Beard, unnoticed, had crept back to his distracted colleague and now loomed behind him. The steel tube of the flashlight crashed own on the kneeling man's head. A second and a third blow followed, then Beard bound the unconscious man with cable ties.

He looked down at his unmoving companion. Then he took the leather wrapper that held the Chronicle and ran back to the entrance, where he placed two explosive charges. He set a timer for fifteen minutes, then quickly made his way back the way they'd come in, checking his watch constantly.

Just as he stepped out of the entrance, he heard the

explosion and the cave-in behind him. Now all he needed were the two last sections of the Chronicle, and the power of King Arthur would be his.

45

ATATÜRK AIRPORT, ISTANBUL

TOM AND EDWARD PASSED THROUGH THE AUTOMATIC doors. From a distance, they saw Vittoria Arcano in the arrivals hall of Istanbul's notoriously overcrowded airport. More than fifty million passengers a year presented a massive organizational challenge for the airport authorities and sometimes exceeded the airport's capacity altogether. Almost fifty percent of all departing flights were delayed. Tom, who had spent a lot of time on planes as an Air Marshal, was therefore extremely surprised when they landed on time, and even more when their bags arrived on the carousel quickly. Tom and Edward had arrived in Geneva late in the evening and boarded the first plane to Istanbul.

After greeting Vittoria, Tom's first question was, "Have you heard anything from Hellen?"

Vittoria nodded. "I called her yesterday. They'd arrived in London. Nothing special to report."

The two men were both relieved to hear it. Tom got straight to the point. "Okay, what do we have? Two dead Blue Shield employees, murdered on a routine support job," he said.

"Yes," Vittoria confirmed, then went on, "They were working with local officials from the Topkapi Palace, examining a find in the cisterns. But no one knows yet exactly what happened."

"I can tell you what happened. The halfwits from the Society of Avalon, a bunch of wannabe knights, murdered them."

Vittoria looked at Tom and Edward in confusion. "Knights? Society of Avalon?" she asked.

Tom and Edward brought her up to date.

"I've already tried to get into to the Topkapi Palace. I wanted to see exactly what they'd found for myself, but they shut me down. Two dead UNESCO officers seems to be enough for them. 'For my own safety,' they said. Chauvinist assholes," Vittoria said angrily.

"Why don't we see if we can find a way in together?" Tom was wearing his lopsided grin, a smile Vittoria knew only too well. "But first we need to put this somewhere very safe." Tom patted his backpack, which contained the leather wrapper containing the section of the Chronicle. "I don't want to carry this around with me, and a hotel safe is a terrible place to put it. A locker here at the airport seems the safest bet to me."

Edward nodded, and they made their way to the lockers. Tom put his backpack inside, dropped in a coin, and secured the locker with a four-digit code, which he shared with Edward and Vittoria. "This way, if anything happens to one of us, the others can still get in. And just in case we get separated, we'll meet back here this evening at eight o'clock."

Vittoria and Edward nodded, and the three of them went to Vittoria's car in the parking garage and drove into the center of Istanbul.

"Why would Istanbul have anything to do with King Arthur?" Tom asked. "Isn't it too far away? I mean, especially back then?"

"Istanbul, under its former name of Constantinople, was the gateway to the East. It was also the capital of the Byzantine Empire for many years, after the fall of Rome. During the Crusades, Constantinople remained an important strategic way station, which meant that many artifacts that the Knights Templar found in Jerusalem ended up being temporarily stored here."

Tom's expression brightened. "I know about that. Hellen told me about it when we were at Lake Como, when we recovered the Shroud of Turin and the other stolen relics. And it wasn't just the Knights Templar helping themselves to the treasures of Jerusalem back then, but the Knights Hospitaler, too."

"Correct," said Edward. "So it seems likely that the Blue Shield guys discovered something that represented a piece of the puzzle for the Society of Avalon. We know they're after the Chronicle of the Round Table, too. And they're not afraid to kill to get it," Edward said.

And I've got AF and Ossana breathing down my neck, too, Tom thought.

"You two make a good team," Vittoria observed as they pulled up near the Topkapi Palace. This time, things went very differently. Vittoria could only suppress a smile as Tom completely overwhelmed the museum director with a torrent of words: his close relationship with the Pope and the U.S. president, a quick reference to the sensational discovery of Kitezh, the earlier affair with all the stolen sacred relics, and the gold of El Dorado—*the man's head must be spinning*, she thought. Overwhelmed, he led them through the palace to the most recent find. Now it was up to Edward to examine the artifacts with the museum's scientific director.

But the find was a waste of time: countless fragments of statues, bits of masonry, and stones from faded mosaics, but nothing of any real significance.

"That's it? That's your sensational find?" Edward said angrily.

Obviously somewhat embarrassed, the scientific director said, "Unfortunately, this is all we've been able to retrieve so far. We had to stop our research in the cisterns when the police came and sealed everything off. The site is now a crime scene. But we are certain there must be far more there, probably even more chambers," the man said apologetically. "But then they found two bodies in the water and the police have to complete their investigations before we can get back in. Forensics, evidence, you know how it is."

Edward nodded, disappointed.

"When do you think we might be able to get in?"

"It could still be quite a while. I know how the police work here, and it could be weeks or even months before the cisterns are open again."

Edward turned to Tom. "We're not going to get anywhere here," he said in annoyance. Tom understood immediately. They had to find a way into the cisterns, and they had to do it before the Society of Avalon could spirit away whatever else was to be found down there. They thanked the scientific director and left the museum.

"I could ask Bayhan if he's had any luck," said Vittoria as they stepped out onto the expanse of the plaza in front of the Topkapi Palace.

"Bayhan? Who's that?" Tom asked.

"He was the local guide for our two colleagues. And he was in the cisterns with them. I spoke to him, and he said he might be able to get us back inside."

"Can we trust him?" Tom asked.

Vittoria tilted her head noncommittally. "I've been wondering that the whole time. Honestly, I don't know for certain, but I think so."

"It's worth a shot. Call him," Tom said.

Two minutes later, it was clear that even Bayhan had been unsuccessful.

"Thank you, Mr. Erdemi, for your efforts. Now only Interpol can help us," she said, and she hung up.

46

THE HAGUE MARKET, THE HAGUE, NETHERLANDS

THE WELSHMAN PUSHED THROUGH THE CROWD WITH HIS bodyguards. Every day, more than twenty-five thousand people visited the Hague Market, which had existed in its present form since 1938. With more than five hundred stalls, the market was one of the biggest multicultural markets in Europe. Exotic food and groceries, antiques and goods foreign, modern, cheap and unique: you could find almost anything at the Hague Market.

The Welshman hated crowds. Why anyone would voluntarily expose themselves to something like this was beyond his comprehension. All the hustle and bustle drove him around the bend.

Here was a stall with Dutch cauliflower, arranged like a still life next to fresh coriander, baklava, persimmons, fresh fish, and black-eyed peas. The next stand sold children's clothes; its neighbor the latest smartphones. If his errand were any less important, wild horses couldn't have dragged him near this place.

They emerged from the parking garage onto Heemstraat and made their way through the labyrinth of market stalls. Jostled and almost bowled over by someone for the fiftieth time, he asked himself angrily why Katalin Farkas wanted to meet him *here*. She had described precisely the exact spice stall where she would be waiting for him. As a signal, he was to buy fifty grams of fenugreek, a hundred grams of ground Indonesian cinnamon, and a tin of tonka beans. He hated this kind of secret-agent crap almost as much as he hated crowds.

He found the stall, waited impatiently until it was his turn, and placed his order. Seconds after he was handed a paper bag with his spices, a woman was standing beside him. She wore a dark headscarf, a bandanna around her neck, and sunglasses.

"Come, Mr. Brice. Walk with me a little," she murmured, and she turned and began to walk toward the exit. They crossed the street and turned onto Marktweg, heading toward Laakkanal. The Welshman's two bodyguards followed at a respectful distance. Katalin kept looking around, her face taut with anxiety.

"We have to be careful. Just after Count Palffy's death, they tried to kill me, too. I know too much . . ."

The Welshman rolled his eyes and hoped the meeting would be worth it. So far, it was looking like no more than the theatrics of an unhinged woman. "My people will look after you," he said, trying to put her more at ease. "They're the best. If your information turns out to have value for me, I'll put a man at your disposal permanently."

He reached into his jacket pocket, took out a thick envelope, and handed it to her. She glanced quickly inside, and her face relaxed noticeably—at least, as far as he could tell behind the headscarf, bandanna, and sunglasses. The sun broke through the gray clouds, warming them a bit as they strolled along the waterfront. This, too, seemed to brighten Katalin's mood, and she relaxed even more. She pushed the scarf back and removed her sunglasses. The Welshman inhaled sharply. She was gorgeous. She looked as if she'd just stepped off the cover of the latest *Vogue*. Her makeup was modest, but in truth her symmetrical features, slightly slanted hazel eyes, small, upturned nose, cheeks—the cold adding a light blush—and full lips really needed no makeup at all. Katalin Farkas was a natural beauty. But judging by her behavior, she was wholly unaware of her effect on him. Which only made her even more attractive.

"I was employed by the count as a housekeeper. My parents came from Hungary originally and fled during the Pan-European Picnic, when the borders opened. My grandfather had worked previously on the Palffy estate, which was how I knew the count. And he gave me a job." She stopped and looked down at the ground. A deep sadness transformed her beautiful face. "But somewhere along the way, I don't remember anymore exactly when it happened, Count Palffy and I developed feelings for each other. We became lovers, but of course no one knew. And of course, he couldn't afford to have anyone find out. The president of Blue Shield in an affair with his young Hungarian housekeeper? Impossible!"

Katalin shook her head and fell silent for a few moments. She was clearly finding it difficult to talk about.

"But that woman, Ossana Ibori, seemed to have a sixth sense. I think she suspected something. Just after Nikolaus's—I mean, the count's—death, she called me and said she wanted to meet. I went to the place we'd agreed to meet, but I stayed back and observed her. My gut feeling told me that she wanted to do something to me. When I returned, my apartment had been turned upside down. That was when I went into hiding."

She had stopped walking and looked into the Welshman's eyes.

"Mr. Brice, Nikolaus mentioned you several times, and I got the impression that you were an upright man, and a man with influence. I had the feeling that he owed you a debt of some kind, which is why I am turning to you now. Because I believe you can help me."

The woman's vulnerability touched the Welshman in a special way. He wanted to take her in his arms and assure her that everything would be all right. But he withstood the urge and instead just laid a consoling hand on her shoulder. She tilted her head a little and, for just a moment, her cheek touched the back of his hand.

"You said you wanted to tell me something important about Count Palffy."

She nodded quickly. "After his death, UNESCO and Interpol both came and searched his house from top to bottom. I was still employed as his housekeeper then. But they did not find his secret chamber."

"Secret chamber?"

"Nikolaus once told me that he had set up a secret room in his basement. I don't know what's in it, but it must be absolutely priceless. He never mentioned it again."

"But you know where this chamber is?" The Welshman furrowed his brow. She nodded again.

"I do. I will gladly tell you everything, but you have to make sure I am safe," Katalin said, taking a step toward him. "Since his death, the house has been put up for sale. I miss the place very much, so I walk by there regularly. The 'for sale' sign is impossible to miss."

"Then we'll simply buy the house," the Welshman said, placing his arm around the young woman's shoulders.

And Katalin knew that, from now on, she would be taken care of.

47

THE "SUBTERRANEAN PALACE," BASILICA CISTERN, ISTANBUL

"Three hundred and thirty-six columns, some more than twenty-five feet high," Edward explained while Vittoria parked the car next to a construction site. "It took seven thousand slaves just a few years to build this architecturally impressive reservoir. This was fifteen hundred years ago, under the Byzantine Empire," he continued, warming enthusiastically to the historical material. "After the fall of the empire, the cistern was buried and forgotten, and not rediscovered until 1545. Today, it's also called the 'Subterranean Palace.'"

"Fascinating, Ducky," Tom interjected.

"Ducky?" Edward asked, surprised.

Vittoria smiled, because she knew what Tom was doing. "NCIS!" she said with a laugh.

"Correct, young padawan. We'll make a proper film nerd out of you yet," Tom said, smiling. His grandfather and he had a game they played: whenever one of them made any kind of reference to a film or series, the other shot back the name of the film, usually within a second or two. And if either one of them got it wrong, they had to buy a round. Vittoria had taken a shine to the old man and had warmed to their game as well.

"She's over there," Vittoria said, waving to Interpol Bureau Chief Nehir Dursun, who was pacing back and forth in front of the cistern, smoking a cigarette.

The three of them crossed the road.

"Thank you for helping us," Vittoria greeted her. Nehir immediately stubbed out the cigarette.

"Sorry, disgusting habit. But this case is wearing on my nerves. It wasn't easy, believe me. But your argument that the killer might return motivated me. Catching him certainly wouldn't hurt my career."

Vittoria made the introductions.

"So what exactly happened?" Tom asked.

Nehir pointed to the construction site across the street. "They were doing construction work here and a passage collapsed. It damaged part of the cistern, but it also revealed the unknown chamber," she explained. "I don't know what you expect to find. There's just an empty room down there. The Topkapi archaeologists already took all of the obvious discoveries away."

"We won't know until we see it for ourselves," said Edward.

"Then what are we waiting for?" Tom said, with a nod to the entrance. They stepped inside the small, unassuming structure that had been set up over the entrance. The reservoir hadn't been properly renovated and opened to the public until the 1980s.

"An attendant was supposed to meet us here to let us in," Nehir said when they were standing in the foyer. "Hello?" she called.

The hair on the back of Tom's neck stood up. Something was wrong. And just as quickly, his sixth sense was proven right. A startled cry escaped Vittoria and they all turned to her.

"I've found him," she said, pointing at the man's body behind the counter.

Tom and Nehir looked over the top of the counter and saw a man with a bullet hole in his head. They looked at each other knowingly and simultaneously drew their guns.

"Foreigners aren't allowed to carry weapons in our country, you know," Nehir warned him.

"And you see how far that got our colleagues. So I asked Vittoria to do us a small favor with her diplomatic luggage."

Vittoria produced her own pistol, too. Nehir screwed up her face.

"Stay behind me, Doc," Tom said. "And do exactly what I say. Understood?"

Edward nodded.

All four descended the long stairway. Despite the danger, Tom couldn't help but notice the beauty of the place. A sea of columns stood in perfect rows in the high vault, which he estimated to be a little larger than a football field. The columns glowed spectrally, lit by orange light. Shallow water shimmering at their bases. Man-made walkways led through the forest of columns.

Looking in all directions and keeping low, they crept along the wooden walkway.

"Why the hell did they go to all the trouble of making the columns so beautiful if they were only planning to flood the place?" Tom asked.

"Because the columns, or at least some of them, were recycled from existing buildings to speed up construction," Edward whispered.

"Boys, could you save the history lesson for later?" Vittoria hissed.

Guns at the ready, they searched the almost 500-foot-long hall. When Tom reached the "Hen's Eye" column, very different from the others and a popular subject for tourist photos, he looked like he was about to ask a question—but a poisonous glare from Vittoria deterred him and he kept his mouth shut.

Suddenly, they heard distant voices and ducked for cover behind the walkway railing. Tom peered in the direction from which he believed the noises had come and saw a few columns surrounded by scaffolding, and a few temporary supports that had been put in place to keep the vault from collapsing.

"They found your men over there, in the water underneath the walkway," Nehir said.

Slowly, trying to stay behind cover, they crept forward to

the corner of the cistern. Now they could see the collapsed section of wall. Additional floodlights had been set up, illuminating the chaos. Part of the side wall had collapsed into the water. One column had fallen and was leaning across the hole in the wall. Police tape marked off the crime scene over a large area.

"You two wait here," Tom said to Edward and Nehir. "Vittoria and I will scope out the situation. Take good care of the doc," he added.

Nehir nodded. "You can count on it."

Without a sound, he and Vittoria slipped into the water, which was only about eighteen inches deep. Wading almost in slow motion, they covered the distance to the huge gap in the wall, restricting their communication to hand signals.

They climbed carefully onto the rubble. The voices were louder now and couldn't be more than a few yards ahead. Once past the pile of rubble, they saw a passage that turned to the right not far ahead. They could hear multiple voices speaking English.

"Pick up the pace, boys. We have to find it ASAP," said a man, whose voice sounded familiar to Tom: it was Sir Lancelot, from the Round Table in Switzerland. At the end of the passage, Tom risked a quick glance around the corner and signaled to Vittoria, who was standing close behind him, that there were three men in the chamber.

"On three," he whispered.

For some inexplicable reason, Vittoria thought of the game Tom and his grandfather played. *But Jesus Christ, this isn't the right time for dumb jokes*, she thought, and just nodded. Tom counted down on his fingers, and they stormed through the narrow entrance.

"Guns down and hands in the air!" Tom bellowed as he and Vittoria strode into the small chamber. The three men turned slowly, hands raised.

"Hail, Sir Lancelot," Tom said with a smirk, and he signaled to him to put his gun on the floor. "Slowly and with two fingers," Tom said emphatically. "You should really think about wearing a mask all the time. Then no one would have to see your shitty face."

The men did as Tom said, placing their pistols and Uzis on the chamber floor.

"Kick them over here," he barked.

Vittoria put her gun away and began to collect the weapons from the floor.

"You can come in," Tom yelled back to Edward and Nehir.

"We're already here," Edward said through gritted teeth.

Before Tom could turn, he heard a sound he knew only too well: the sound of a pistol being cocked.

48

GRAND HOTEL EXCELSIOR VITTORIA, SORRENTO, GULF OF NAPLES, ITALY

CLOUTARD SIGHED AS HE STEPPED OUT ONTO THE HOTEL terrace. If there was a heaven on earth anywhere, this must be it. The roofed terrace with its glorious arches offered a truly breathtaking view over the Gulf of Naples. Mount Vesuvius loomed on the horizon, and more than a few luxury boats bobbed in the gulf below. An enormous ocean liner was just edging into Sorrento Harbor.

The Grand Hotel Excelsior Vittoria sat atop a sheer cliff high above the town. A great many celebrities had resided there in the past: the Austrian Empress Elisabeth, Marilyn Monroe, Richard Wagner, Princess Margaret, Luciano Pavarotti. And although Cloutard loved Venice, he believed the famous quotation should have been reworded: "see Sorrento and die" made more sense to him.

Thorvald Brix sat at the end of the terrace in a wicker chair and gazed out contentedly over the gulf. When he saw Cloutard, he stood up, came to him, and embraced him with surprising warmth.

"Thank you, François. Thank you for giving me back my old life. I was getting as dusty as all the old books in that damned library." He turned around and pointed out over the sea. "This is what I was born for. Not for pushing moldy books from point A to point B." But he quickly returned to business. "You have my fee?" he asked, narrowing his eyes at Cloutard.

Cloutard nodded and patted the briefcase, which he held up in his left hand. "Let's go to your suite," he said. "I hope everything has been arranged as usual."

Brix nodded. "The hotel management has been as obliging as ever. My workplace is just as it used to be. The materials were already waiting for me when I arrived."

"You mean you already have something I can see?"

Brix nodded again. "You know me, François. Give me inspiring surroundings and I not only do perfect work, I do it quickly."

They took the elevator up to Brix's suite. Cloutard knew great hotels all around the world. But every time he stepped into a suite at the Grand Hotel Excelsior Vittoria, it took his breath away. Only the Italians could get away with this level of pomp, opulence, almost over-the-top luxury.

Brix was staying in the Caruso suite, which the hotel had turned into a small atelier for him. The sumptuous sofa and armchairs had been replaced by an easel and other tools of the counterfeiter's trade, but the alterations did not detract at all from the stylish ambience of the room.

The large mirror hanging above the open fireplace added an extra dimension to the already generous room. Light-colored floral wallpaper, an antique free-standing screen, expensive carpets, an antique piano. Real candles flanked the music stand, and original photographs of Enrico Caruso decorated the walls. But the absolute highlight of the suite was surely the balcony. One could drink in the view for hours.

Cloutard admired the work Brix had already done.

"I am impressed, Thorvald. You have been working very quickly indeed."

"It's like I said. All I need is the right environment."

Cloutard went out onto the terrace and stood gazing over the sea. Brix followed him out.

"What would you say if I said I had more work for you?"

Brix looked at Cloutard with a mixture of enthusiasm and astonishment.

"If I can stay here, then yes. Whatever the work involves."

"There will, however, be a small change in the payment arrangements. We will not be paying you in advance for your services, but instead offering you a percentage of what we make when we sell."

Brix raised one eyebrow dubiously. He was an artist, not a businessman. He was not used to this kind of deal. He was paid for the work he did. He preferred it that way: it was safer. Cloutard recognized the Dane's doubts instantly.

"It's about 'The Storm on the Sea of Galilee' and 'The

Concert.'"

Brix's mouth dropped open. It took him a few seconds to recover himself.

"*You* were behind the Boston job? You've got the Rembrandt and the Vermeer?" His voice failed him—he could speak only in a whisper.

A proud smile spread across Cloutard's face. It was nice to finally reveal himself as the one who had pulled off that masterpiece of burglary. He nodded.

"And you're planning to sell them on the black market? The originals or my reproductions?"

Clearly, Brix had accepted the job already, at least mentally.

"That is yet to be clarified. We need a good strategy concerning the best approach to take, both with the original and with your masterpieces. We have to think it through thoroughly."

Cloutard reached out his hand to Brix.

"Deal?"

"One moment, François."

Brix returned to the room and came back moments later with two cognac glasses.

"Louis XIII?" Cloutard asked.

"What else?" said Brix.

The glasses clinked as the two men toasted their extremely lucrative partnership.

49

BURIAL CHAMBER, CISTERNA BASILICA, ISTANBUL

TOM TURNED AROUND SLOWLY. HE THOUGHT BRIEFLY about trying something, but Nehir Dursun had her finger on the trigger of her pistol, which she held pressed to the back of Edward's head, and she looked nervous. Vittoria dropped the thugs' weapons, and the three men instantly pounced on them. Tom held his gun in two fingers and raised his hands. He couldn't risk Edward's life in a foolhardy rescue attempt.

"On your knees!" Lancelot rushed at Tom, grabbed his pistol and forced him to the chamber floor. "Tie them up!" he ordered his companions.

"Why are you doing this?" Vittoria asked. "Haven't enough people died already?"

"Shut your mouth. I have no intention of justifying myself to you. Do what he said! On your knees, or you can add one more to the list of bodies," Nehir said, and she jammed her gun harder into Edward's head.

"Better do as she says," Tom said. Vittoria went down on her knees and held her hands out toward one of the men to tie them. Moments later, Tom and Vittoria lay in a corner like two well-trussed bundles.

"Now we come to you, Dr. de Mey. You're going to help us find the Chronicle, or things are going to get very uncomfortable for your two friends here," Lancelot said, planting himself in front of Edward, who was also on his knees now, his hands clasped on top of his head.

"And if you come up empty-handed, you'll end up like your daughter," Nehir added.

Edward spun around and tried to stand up. "Hellen?" he cried, but Lancelot swung his fist and Edward hit the floor. Tom struggled to break his bonds. A sharp, electric pain had shot through his body at Nehir's words. A tear slid down Vittoria's cheek.

"What have you done to Hellen?" Tom snapped.

"Oh, does she mean something special to you?"

"If you've done anything to her, you're dead."

"Mr. Wagner, how could *I* have done anything to her? No, I just saw the news at my office—something about a UNESCO employee in London shot full of holes and fighting for her life in intensive care." Nehir crouched in front of Tom and pinched his cheek. Tom recoiled in disgust. "But it doesn't look good. I'd hold off on the wedding plans, if I were you."

She straightened up and turned to Lancelot. "Do what you have to do, then let's get out of here. The local police could come back any time."

Lancelot grabbed Edward by the arm and dragged him to his feet. "Where's the damned Chronicle?"

"What do you want from me? How should I know where it is? The only reason we're here is because you happened to mention it in Switzerland."

Edward's voice was cracking. He was having trouble forming clear thoughts. All he could think of was Hellen.

"Stay focused, Doc," Tom said reassuringly. "Hellen's strong. She'll come through. And you'll get through this, too. Go through the facts. Take your time." Inside, he was struggling too. He couldn't know if Hellen would really make it—but this was what Edward needed to hear right now, or they were all lost. Everything was in his hands. Tom had been trained to keep his emotions in check, but he could see that Edward was close to breaking down. "You can do it, Doc."

Edward cleared his throat. He thought for a moment and recited the facts he knew could be relevant. "Constantinople was once the hub between East and West, strategically crucial in the Crusades. For centuries, the Crusaders, and of course the Templars, once known as the Knights of the Round Table"—he looked at Lancelot —"transported priceless treasures from the Holy Land through Constantinople to the West."

"Thank you, we know all that. Get to the point," Lancelot said.

Carefully, keeping his hands raised, Edward began moving slowly through the room, looking all around. He was gradually calming down. Talking about the historical background distracted him from the sad reality, and he went deeper into the history.

"There must be hundreds of knights' graves still undiscovered here in Istanbul, as Constantinople is known today. They were often laid to rest in small, underground burial chambers—or, if they were financially better-off, they would have a place in a larger crypt. There was once a basilica on top of these cisterns, too, which is where the name "Cisterna Basilica" comes from. So it would make sense for burial chambers or sections of the crypt to be very close by. The walls here certainly suggest that."

Edward was standing in front of a wall, and he swept his hand over the brick surface. The low vault measured about twenty feet square, with small niches carved into the sides. At the front of the vault there had once been a statue in a recess in the wall, but all that remained now was the plinth and the eroded stumps of feet. Presumably, the rest of the statue had been taken to the Topkapi Palace with the rubble.

Edward took in every detail. He brushed aside cobwebs, wiped away dust, looked at everything.

"What's taking so long? Maybe you didn't take our warning seriously enough, eh?" Lancelot said, and he turned and pointed his gun at Vittoria.

"Dr. de Mey, please!" Vittoria begged.

"Wait!" Edward shouted. He was on his knees in front of one of the plinths now, blowing away the dust of centuries. "I've found something."

Lancelot lowered his pistol and went over to the niche. Edward pointed to the area around the feet of the statue, atop the stone base. The feet were mounted on a second stone slab, which was not quite in the center of the plinth and slightly tilted. Nothing about it stood out at first glance, certainly not when it was covered with a thick layer of sand and dust. Across the face of the plinth, part of an inscription was visible.

"Baphomet," Edward murmured.

"What? Baphomet?"

"Here, look. You can't really see all of it, but unless I'm very much mistaken, this says 'TEM OHP AB.' Or read the other way: 'Baphomet.' It's an ananym, derived from 'templi omnium hominum pacis abbas,' or 'abbot of the temple of peace of all men,' which alludes to the Templars' connection to the Temple of Solomon. Baphomet was an idol mentioned in the transcripts of the Inquisition of the Knights Templar as early as 1307. The Knights Templar were supposed to have worshipped Baphomet, or at least, that's what they say."

"You've found it. We're in the right place!" Lancelot cried. "Come on, help him," he said, waving over his men.

"We need to center the baseplate on the plinth."

The two men grabbed hold of the remains of the statue's feet and pushed. Slowly, accompanied by a lot of grating and scraping, they shifted the heavy slab across the plinth until it locked into place with a loud "clack."

They heard a rumbling inside the wall, and suddenly the back of the niche banged loudly and moved backward about an inch. Air hissed through the newly formed gap.

50

ADVOCATUUR TAMMERVELD & VAN DALFSEN, ZORGVLIET DISTRICT, THE HAGUE

KATALIN FARKAS HAD SLIPPED HER ARM INTO THE Welshman's as they exited the car and, accompanied by two bodyguards, they entered one of the many brick buildings along Johan-de-Wittlaan-Allee arm in arm.

The Zorgvliet district of The Hague, also known as the "international zone," was home to the International Criminal Court, the Organization for the Prohibition of Chemical Weapons, Europol, the World Forum Convention Center, and the Peace Palace, which housed the Permanent Court of Arbitration, among other notable institutions. But because of the importance of these organizations to Europe and the world, a profusion of lobbying and consulting firms had also sprung up in the area, along with law firms, pharmaceutical companies, and embassies. Here and there, an establishment of a more dubious sort had put down roots as well.

Katalin Farkas seemed reborn. She was radiant, confident, her beauty accentuated by a new designer dress—

one of a number of items Berlin Brice had bought for her in the Scheveningen shopping district. Hardly a man she passed did not feel drawn to her.

They stepped into the spacious rooms of the Tammerveld & van Dalfsen legal firm. Jan-Willem van Dalfsen met them personally and led them to a conference room with a stunning view over Zorgfliet Park.

"How's it look, Jan?" the Welshman asked once the usual greetings and small talk were out of the way. "What have you found out?"

"Count Palffy's death is a strange case. The police here in The Hague did investigate, but their investigation was completed unusually fast, and the case was filed away. That would have been strange behavior even with an everyday murder, but it's a whole lot stranger when you're talking about Count Palffy—the president of Blue Shield, a UNESCO organization—but regardless, the investigation uncovered nothing. UNESCO itself cleaned the house out quickly, and there's been nothing ever since. Even the press has been silent—the international newspapers barely mentioned the story. Palffy's post was quickly taken over by a woman named Theresia de Mey, and the case was closed."

Katalin squeezed the Welshman's hand. "It's just like I told you."

"My sources get extremely cautious whenever this particular subject is raised. It's as if they're afraid of something," the lawyer went on. "I have a Europol informant who even mentioned a terrorist organization that goes by the name of Absolute Freedom, or something like that.

Apparently, they're implicated in all kinds of nasty business around the world."

Brice had listened to his lawyer in silence. "All right. And what about the house?"

"No good news, I'm afraid," the lawyer said with a sigh. "It was sold a few weeks ago to the CEO of a rather shady lobbying firm, a Lithuanian named Kristo Skudra. Suspected links to one of the many criminal cliques that sprang up after the USSR fell apart."

Katalin looked in horror at Berlin. All her hopes were vanishing before her eyes. If she wasn't able to show him what he wanted to see, he would quickly lose interest in her. Their lovemaking the night before would make no difference, she feared. A man like the Welshman could have any number of beautiful women. Her ace in the hole was Palffy's "secret chamber."

"Then we should—what do they say these days?—*reach out* to this Mr. Skudra with a lucrative offer of our own," the Welshman said.

"I already have," van Dalfsen said. "But unsuccessfully. His lawyer made it very clear that the house is not for sale."

The Welshman did not seem daunted by this news. "If money won't do the job, then we'll simply have to find another way to persuade him. What weak points does he have?"

"Two daughters. They live with their mother in Riga. The couple divorced about five years ago."

Brice nodded with satisfaction. "Then we know what's to

be done. Do you have someone who can take care of it? Or should I send one of mine?"

The lawyer shook his head. "Absolutely not, Mr. Brice. You don't need to do a thing. Of course we'll take care of that for you. I have a former SAS man who is very reliable."

"I would think that an argument that convincing would also encourage Mr. Skudra to ask a very reasonable price," Brice said casually.

Van Dalfsen smiled. "Most certainly."

"It might also be advisable to remove Mr. Skudra from the picture completely once the sale has gone through. We really don't want anyone around who might interfere in our future dealings."

The Welshman's tone made it very clear that it was not just a suggestion but an irrevocable instruction. Katalin Farkas had her work cut out maintaining a poker face when she heard this exchange. She was starting to realize the kind of people she had gotten herself mixed up with —and she loved it. She loved being at the side of a man with authority and influence. The Welshman's cruelty was a powerful aphrodisiac.

Brice was on his feet and shaking the lawyer's hand.

"We'll be here in The Hague a few more days. I'd like to have the matter settled quickly."

The lawyer nodded. "Of course, Mr. Brice. I'll be in touch as soon as I have the key. I'll handle the sale using the power of attorney you've already signed."

The Welshman and Katalin Farkas left the office. "Let's go back to the hotel and celebrate," she whispered in his ear.

51

"Push! Come on!" Lancelot urged his men.

The two men heaved, and the massive stone block moved inward, enlarging the gap far enough for a person to squeeze through.

"Dr. de Mey, if you would be so kind," Lancelot said, gesturing toward the newly opened gap invitingly. Edward moved toward Lancelot and the gap but glanced back briefly at Tom and Vittoria.

Lancelot glowered at his men. "You guys stay here. Make sure those two don't do anything stupid," he said. He snapped on a flashlight and handed it to Edward, then followed the older man through.

An excited tingle ran through Edward as he stepped into the chamber behind the niche. For a moment, he forgot everything around him and simply soaked in the magnificence that welcomed them on the other side. He was the first human being in centuries to cross the threshold of this low, vaulted chamber. He knew he was in the right place, suddenly much closer to his goal. Three stone sarcophagi stood close together in front of them. He swung the flashlight around wildly, not knowing where to start.

"Give me a few minutes," Edward asked. He stepped up beside the first sarcophagus and studied the beautifully carved relief on its lid. The figure reclining atop each of the stone coffins represented the knight interred within. They reminded Edward of the marble effigies in Temple Church in London. Almost tenderly, Edward swept his hand across the ancient stone, covered lightly with dust and sand.

"This is fantastic! I have never seen a Templar burial site this well preserved. Who were they, I wonder?" Edward said, mostly to himself.

"Dr. de Mey, I'm glad you appreciate my forefathers so much, but right now we have more pressing things to do than answer romantic archaeological questions. Find the Chronicle, or you'll soon be joining these men."

"What do you expect from me? I have to study these sarcophagi in peace. It will take time."

"Time is exactly what we don't have."

Lancelot went back outside for a moment and returned with a huge sledgehammer. "Stand aside," he said.

"Nooo! For God's sa—," Edward screamed. But he was too late. With two solid blows of the big hammer, Lancelot smashed the first of the three stone lids. He hauled the broken pieces heedlessly onto the floor.

"That lid might have contained clues! You're destroying

centuries-old cultural relics," Edward stammered in disbelief.

"Shut up and search the sarcophagus." A few more swings of the hammer and Lancelot had smashed the other sarcophagus lids, too. He dropped the hammer onto the chamber floor.

"I . . . I can't. You're destroying everything," Edward said with a sigh of despair.

The knights' facial features, recognizable at first, fell instantly to dust when exposed to the air by Lancelot's violence. All that remained were bones and the metal of their armor.

"Fuck! There's nothing here," Lancelot swore, once he'd gone through all three sarcophagi like a berserker.

He stormed at Edward, grabbed him by his collar and slammed him hard against the wall. "Where's the fucking scroll?" he screamed at the archaeologist. Fear and desperation resonated in his voice.

"I don't know. You've destroyed almost everything that might have given us a clue!"

A hard punch to the face knocked Edward to the floor. Boiling over with anger, Lancelot paced through the chamber before rifling through the sarcophagi again. Grimacing with pain, Edward opened his eyes and found himself looking at the foot section of one of the sarcophagi, which stood raised from the ground on four huge lion's paws. And then he stared: in the center between the feet, he recognized a symbol carved in relief. He pulled himself together and looked at it more closely.

The relief showed a head with three faces, but it stood upside down. Edward had only recognized it at all because he was lying on the floor when he saw it.

He wheezed the word he'd said earlier: "Baphomet." He reached out his hand and ran his fingers over the relief, which was circular and about four inches in diameter. "I've got something!" he groaned, more loudly, and Lancelot hurried over. "This symbol . . . it's also in the Templar fortress in Tomar, Portugal, and it's known in a number of circles as a representation of Baphomet. But it's upside down."

"And what does that tell you?"

Without answering, Edward grasped the relief with both hands and twisted with all his strength. Bit by bit, the disk turned. Lancelot's impatience grew with every tiny movement. A click. Edward pressed on the symbol and a compartment opened on the underside of the coffin. Lancelot pushed Edward aside roughly and grabbed at the clay cylinder that had appeared in the compartment.

"No! Wait!" Edward cried, but Lancelot had already smashed the sealed container on the edge of the sarcophagus. Inside was a familiar leather wrapper, which he inspected with satisfaction.

"What's taking so long in there? We have to get out of here," Nehir called. "The police are on their way. I've just heard it on the scanner. Someone called them."

Lancelot grabbed Edward by the collar and forced him back through the opening into the outer chamber. He pushed him onto the floor in front of Tom.

"We're done here. Kill them," he ordered his men, who instantly raised their guns.

"Stop!" Tom cried.

"What now?"

"Don't you want to know where we've hidden the section of the Chronicle we snatched from you in Switzerland?" Tom asked. It was a gamble. He had no intention of actually telling Lancelot where he'd hidden it, but he had to win some time. He could not lose track of the third section, the one that Lancelot was now holding, and there was no way he could let his friends die for it.

"I can lead you to it, but in return you have to let my friends live."

"Tom, no. You can't," Vittoria objected.

But Tom ignored her. "I'll go with you, and you leave my friends here. Then I'll give you your piece back. Everyone's happy, everyone wins, everyone lives. Deal?"

Lancelot thought for a moment. Nehir's radio crackled again, and a Turkish voice barked instructions.

"We're out of time," she said, already heading for the exit when Lancelot finally spoke up.

"Okay. Tie the old man up and let's get out of here." Lancelot hauled Tom to his feet and dragged him out. Tom and Edward exchanged a final look.

Back in the cistern, Nehir was already a ways ahead. She definitely wanted to avoid meeting the local police.

"Go ahead and bring the car around," Lancelot ordered one of his men. Then he turned to Tom. "By the way, I have to tell you that your performance at our headquarters was extremely impressive."

But Tom remained silent all the way back to the stairs. He had a plan, and he didn't want to get distracted now by small talk.

But when they were halfway up the stairs, a shot rang out.

52

CISTERNA BASILICA, ISTANBUL

"Stop where you are! Don't move!" one of the officers yelled. He looked nervous. It wasn't every day that he got to draw his pistol on a public street and take cover behind his patrol car. The four officers had parked their cars across the middle of the street, blocking it completely, and were crouched behind them. Passersby, panicked by the gunshot, were hiding behind cars or running away.

The officers had their guns trained on the woman who had just stepped from the Cisterna Basilica ticket office into the open air.

"Don't shoot! I'm from Interpol," Nehir Dursun shouted. She took a few steps forward, her hands in the air. She held her Interpol ID in one hand and her pistol in the other and kept glancing back nervously over her shoulder.

"That's her," said Bayhan Erdemi to one of the policemen. "She can't be allowed to escape."

"Stop where you are! Down on the ground!" the officer shouted at Nehir from the relative safety of his patrol car.

"I'm with Interpol," Nehir shouted back, waving her ID.

"Put your gun down. It's over," Bayhan ordered her.

Very slowly, Nehir went down on her knees.

"When the hell is our backup getting here?" Bayhan muttered.

Nehir was still holding her ID high in the air. With the other hand, she laid her pistol on the ground.

"Stay on your knees!" Bayhan shouted. "Hands behind your head." He kept his gun pointed at Nehir, aiming carefully.

"They're in there. They've got guns and hostages," Nehir called.

Just then, another shot cracked. Bayhan and the policemen ducked. A red mist burst from Nehir Dursun's chest. She toppled face-first onto the ground and lay without moving.

———

"The bitch double-crossed us," Lancelot snarled as he lowered his pistol and ducked into cover beside the window. He stared at the dead body of the man Nehir had killed, lying in the middle of the ticket office lobby. "Shit, shit, shit!" He kicked and punched at the walls, beside himself with anger.

"What do we do now?" his remaining sidekick asked, nervously tapping the floor with his foot. He was holding so tightly to his Uzi that his knuckles had turned white.

"You could give up. How about that?" Tom said with a chuckle, crouching on the floor almost disinterestedly beside the two men.

"You just keep your damned mouth shut." Lancelot went to Tom and jammed his gun into Tom's forehead.

"Remember what you want from me. As first knight, you gotta deliver," Tom jibed, calmly staring up the barrel of Lancelot's pistol.

"AAARRGGHHH," Lancelot screamed. He jerked his gun away and paced through the lobby, banging the gun against his own forehead as he went. "I have to think!"

"Put down your weapons and come out with your hands up," a voice from outside droned. The police had found a megaphone.

Lancelot stopped pacing. "Run back down and bring up his friends. The bitch was right. We have hostages."

The other man nodded and got to his feet. As he ran past Tom toward the stairs, Tom jumped to his feet and rammed a knife into his kidney: the same knife Edward had passed to him when they'd pushed him to the floor at Tom's feet earlier. The man opened his mouth in a silent scream and collapsed.

Tom swung the limp body around, drawing the man's pistol from his belt holster as he turned, firing in Lancelot's direction. But it was an awkward position, the man's body was heavy and accurate targeting was impossible. The bullets flew wide. And Lancelot was fast. He leaped behind the counter, squeezing off two shots as he jumped. They were on target, but his partner's body shielded Tom from injury.

"It's over!" Tom shouted. "Give it up."

"A true knight never surrenders," Lancelot bellowed back.

Tom rolled his eyes and shook his head. *These guys aren't playing with a full deck*, he thought, pushing the pistol into his belt. He grabbed the Uzi his human shield still held in his hands, pushed the lifeless body aside, ducked and ran across to the near side of the counter.

Lancelot suddenly jumped to his feet, grabbed hold of the office chair and used it to smash the window behind the counter. Tom raised the Uzi and squeezed off a short burst as Lancelot dropped back into cover.

"Just give me the Chronicle and I'll let you go," Tom said.

"Oh, you'd like that, wouldn't you? Come and get it." With that, Lancelot jumped up, firing several shots to keep Tom down, and leaped out through the shattered window.

Tom looked up in time to see Lancelot's feet disappearing outside. He vaulted over the counter, jumped through the window, and went after him.

53

KAPALI ÇARŞI (GRAND BAZAAR), ISTANBUL

Sirens wailed through the streets of Istanbul. Tom ran for all he was worth, the cold air burning in his lungs. He couldn't let Lancelot escape—Edward's life depended on it.

Once they'd cleared the small section of trees behind the ticket office, they ran east, Lancelot plowing his way along the busy street, jostling and pushing his way through cursing passersby.

Fifty yards ahead, a streetcar was just pulling to a stop. Passengers began to disembark and others boarded. Lancelot ran past all of them and sprang into the front section of the train at the last second. Tom reached the other end just in time to get aboard before the doors closed.

He forced his way forward through the crowded streetcar until he saw Lancelot ahead. The two men glared at each other, fingers on their triggers, but they kept their guns out of sight. They could not finish it in here. They stood in front of their respective doors, their eyes glued to one another.

Tom was ready. Somewhere along the line, Lancelot would have to get off, and then he had him. He glanced up at an advertisement as they passed, and suddenly knew what Lancelot had in mind. The Grand Bazaar of Istanbul, Kapalı Çarşı. The world's oldest bazaar, and one of the most visited tourist attractions anywhere—a mazelike structure covering 37,000 square yards, full of tiny shops and throngs of people. The perfect place to disappear. Tom was suddenly a lot less confident.

The streetcar slowed and stopped. The doors slid open, and Lancelot took off running, Tom close behind, the two men zigzagging through the tight alleys dodging count-less locals and tourists. Tom was overwhelmed by the array of colors, smells, and sounds. Carpets, spices, jewelry, clothes, souvenirs, lamps. The red flag of Turkey, with its half-moon and star, hung everywhere.

Lancelot kept looking back over his shoulder, and Tom struggled not to lose sight of him. Like an Olympic swim-mer, he fought ahead through the masses. *How am I supposed to get my hands on him in this crowd?*

Lancelot turned sharply and ran in the direction of the Eski Bedesten—"the old cloth market," situated in the center of the bazaar. Originally designed in the 15th century under Sultan Mehmed Fatih as a treasure cham-ber, it later served as a bank. Today, the beautifully deco-rated vaults of the Eski Bedesten were mainly home to jewelry dealers, interspersed with many other shops. A visitor here could feel themselves catapulted back to another time, with modern stores rubbing shoulders with traditional market stalls.

Two policemen were standing at the entrance to the historical market hall. Lancelot saw them and changed direction, trying to avoid drawing their attention—but it was too late. A glance back over his shoulder told Tom that two new players had joined the game. The two officers were close behind him and Lancelot, and they looked intent on stopping the two troublemakers. Suddenly, Lancelot disappeared down a narrow passage between buildings. Tom abruptly changed direction to follow, knocking a man over.

"Sorry," Tom shouted over his shoulder as he turned into the passage after Lancelot. But he stopped in surprise. Where was the man? It was as if he'd vanished into thin air. Then Tom heard a cry and saw the small door. He ran to it and tore it open. On the other side, a narrow stairway led upward, and Tom disappeared through the door just as the cops came racing around the corner.

Now Tom saw where the cry had come from. A young woman was sitting on the stairs, massaging her ankle. She recoiled as Tom hurried past and he realized that Lancelot must have pushed her out of the way. He heard the sound of breaking glass, and took the stairs two at a time. Seconds later, he climbed out through the broken window and onto the roof to see Lancelot fleeing across the rooftops against a breathtaking vista: hundreds of buildings built so close together that it looked like a brick-red landscape of hills dotted with dormers, skylights and fans. Here and there, one building projected higher than the others. Tom ran. He would catch him now. Roof tiles cracked under his feet as he darted from ridge to ridge. He slid down sloping valleys, jumped over air conditioners, dodged satellite dishes, and narrowly avoided getting hung up on TV antennas.

Then he saw his chance and took it. He raised his pistol and fired. A hit. Lancelot fell.

54

CISTERNA BASILICA, ISTANBUL

"Seal everything off, get forensics in here, call Interpol, block the street." Bayhan was in the ticket office now, barking one order after another. More police had arrived in the meantime, and now that the danger had been neutralized, they had their hands full keeping the gawkers on the street under control. "Search every corner of the cistern, especially the room where the artifacts were found."

"*Peki efendim.*" Several officers immediately ran down to the cistern.

What the hell happened here? Bayhan went over to one corner of the ticket office and tried to make sense of the scene. He counted three bodies inside. A cistern employee, presumably killed by the intruders. A man that, he assumed, Nehir had shot—*that was the shot I heard when I first arrived*, he thought. *The second shot was the one that killed Nehir, before all hell broke loose in here. But who killed the third man? And who escaped through the window?*

Bayhan moved through the scene carefully. He inspected the bullet holes in the walls, the positions of the bodies, the shattered window. *Was there an argument among the criminals? What happened here?* He could not work it out.

His radio crackled to life.

"We've found two hostages in the sealed-off section. They're alive."

"Good. Bring them up. I want to talk to them."

A short time later, the officers led Edward de Mey and Vittoria Arcano upstairs.

"Bayhan?" Vittoria said in surprise. "What are you doing here? You're—"

Bayhan was wearing more or less the same plain, nondescript clothes he'd been wearing when he and Vittoria first met. The difference now was the police badge dangling from a chain around his neck. He held it up.

"A cop, yes. Undercover."

Vittoria smiled.

"And you must be Dr. de Mey," Bayhan said, holding out his hand to Edward.

"You got here just in time. Thank you," Edward said.

"I guess you can't . . ." But Bayhan left the sentence unfinished. "No. How could you?"

"What?" Vittoria asked.

"You can't explain to me what happened here, can you?" He swept his hands wide, encompassing the chaos around them.

Vittoria smiled again. "I wasn't here, but I have a pretty good idea what happened," she said, and she looked happily at Edward.

"Tom!" they both said.

"Tom?"

"Tom Wagner. He also works, or used to work, for Blue Shield. We actually thought he was dead, but then he wasn't and—" Vittoria interrupted herself and raised her hands in surrender. "That would take too long now. But he's one of the good guys. And because he's not here, it means he's probably after the guy who was leading these bastards. These guys are all his accomplices."

"This is going to mean a ton of paperwork," Bayhan sighed.

An officer approached. "Forensics just arrived," he said to Bayhan, who nodded.

"Let's go out and let my colleagues get to work. I need to get statements from both of you, and then I'll take you to your hotel."

Vittoria and Edward followed him outside.

"Whoa!" Vittoria exclaimed when she saw Nehir's body lying out front of the ticket office.

"At least *she* got what she deserved."

"Vittoria!" Edward chided, shaking his head disapprovingly.

"Sorry." She turned to Bayhan. "So, what do you have to do with any of this? You're obviously not a tour guide."

"I work for . . . a kind of white-collar crime department, I guess you'd call it. We focus on the illegal trade in art and antiquities. Nehir Dursun was on my radar for a long time, but I could never pin anything on her. But when your two Blue Shield agents turned up dead, Nehir suddenly showed a lot of interest in the case. And when you told me you wanted to ask Interpol for help, my alarm bells really started ringing."

"In any case, we're eternally grateful that you came when you did. You saved our asses."

"Vittoria!"

"Saved our *lives*. Sorry. I'm just so happy to be out of there."

55

THE ROOFTOPS OF THE GRAND BAZAAR, ISTANBUL

"GODDAMMIT," TOM MUTTERED WHEN LANCELOT'S BODY dropped below his field of view.

He ran on, slowing only when he drew close to the spot where Lancelot had disappeared. Seven feet below was a small, level space, a kind of terrace. An air conditioner hummed, and market noises from the bazaar rose from below. No sign of Lancelot. Tom slipped warily down from the roof, pistol at the ready.

Without warning, Lancelot jumped from a hiding place and tackled Tom, and they hit the terrace hard. Tom's gun was knocked from his hand and slipped over the edge. Grappling and punching, they rolled across the narrow terrace and crashed onto a tiled roof a few feet lower. A sharp edge dug into Tom's back, and pain shot through him. Lancelot produced a dagger and stabbed at Tom's neck, but Tom was able to block it in time. The dagger hovered, quivering just above his throat, while Tom's free hand scrabbled for anything he could use as a weapon. Finally, his fingers found a shard of broken tile and he rammed it into Lancelot's side, making him bellow in pain. Now it was Tom's turn. He heaved the injured man off him, then threw himself on top and punched Lancelot in the head until he stopped moving. Completely exhausted, Tom rolled to the side and lay there for a moment to catch his breath.

He'd done it. He struggled to his knees and hunted through the unconscious Lancelot's pockets. Inside his jacket, he found what he was looking for: the leather wrapper containing the last part of the Chronicle of the Round Table.

Just then, a bullet whizzed past his head and slammed into the sloping roof beside him. Pigeons scattered from under the roof. Tom ducked.

"*Dur polis*. Do not move. Police!" he heard someone shout across the rooftops.

"Shoot first, ask questions later. Whatever works, I guess," Tom murmured to himself, peeking over the ridge of the roof. He grabbed Lancelot's pistol and fired two shots into the air—he wasn't about to get caught in a shootout with the police, not here and now. He had enough problems to deal with. The police took cover, and Tom was up and running. Keeping low, he ran for his life, scuttling on all fours up the slope of a roof and sliding down the other side. More shots rang out, and tiles exploded around him.

These guys aren't screwing around, he thought. He slid down another roof. Dead end: a sheer drop, no way forward. His eyes darted around and found the only route open to him. He jumped, just managing to grab a cable stretched across the yard below. The sudden jolt ripped one end of the cable free. He fell, desperately hanging on, and swung into the wall of the building. He pushed away and to one side, then swung in again, this time with his feet in front and aiming for a window. It smashed under the force of his swing, and he let go of the cable as he passed through and rolled clear. It was a move he'd practiced a hundred times with Cobra, his former special forces unit.

He was in an old storeroom. Hurting everywhere, he limped through the rooms, following the noise from the bazaar. It grew louder and louder, and he soon found the exit. He was safe, and he vanished into the crowd like a ghost.

56

ATATÜRK AIRPORT, ISTANBUL

HOURS LATER, EDWARD AND VITTORIA WERE FINALLY DONE with their statements at Bayhan's station, and at their request he had organized a ride for them to the airport. It was just before eight p.m., and they strode purposefully through the busy terminal heading directly for the lockers.

"I'm a little concerned that we haven't heard from Tom. Do you think something's happened to him?" Vittoria asked.

"Don't worry. I've seen what he's capable of, and I'm confident he'll be here on time." They stopped for a moment and Edward swung an arm around Vittoria and gently squeezed her shoulder. "Why the sudden doubt? You did great today."

"I belong back at my desk."

"But why? Theresia told me that you've been pestering her for months about working in the field."

"But if I had stuck to the rules, we would never have been in that situation."

"Yes, but we'd also be standing here empty-handed. Don't worry, please. You did fine."

"We'd better hurry. It's nearly eight," Vittoria said, and they started walking again.

A few minutes later, they reached the lockers. "Here it is," Vittoria said, knocking on one of them. "Do you remember the code?"

"Of course," he said, and recited the numbers Tom had shared with them earlier.

"Shouldn't we wait for Tom?" Vittoria said. She had been about to type in the code, but hesitated.

"Why? Let's go and sit in that café. Then I can at least study it while we're waiting."

Vittoria nodded and tapped in the code.

"I don't think Tom's coming . . ." Vittoria said, her voice blank, when she swung open the door.

"Vittoria, don't be so nega—" Edward had stepped up behind her, and what he saw choked the word in his throat. They looked at one another in incomprehension. The locker in which part of the Chronicle of the Round Table had been lying just a few hours before was empty.

57

TABARKA FORTRESS, TUNISIA, TWO WEEKS LATER

IT HAD BEEN A FULL YEAR SINCE THE FIRST TIME TOM HAD followed the curving road that led to the sand-colored fortress. Since that day, his life had changed fundamentally. A year ago, he had been bored to death of his job with Cobra, but now he had all the action and excitement he could handle. But there was another difference, too: back then, his boundaries had been more clearly defined; he had known which side he was on. Now, he was operating in a gray area. The boundary between good and evil was no longer as clear.

The gate to François Cloutard's former base swung open as he drew near. He was expected. This, in fact, was where good and evil had first begun to blur—where he and François had joined forces and fought on the same side. And the Frenchman, ever since, had proven himself not only a good friend but also an invaluable member of his team.

His team . . . could he ever go back to his old life, the life from which he'd been torn so violently? Could he just pick up the pieces and keep going? Or had he already stepped too far over the line?

The entrance hall was dominated by massive pillars and a huge staircase. Two men came to meet him there, and one of them patted him down for weapons.

"Welcome to Tabarka," he heard Ossana call as she descended the majestic stairway.

"I see you've done some work on the place," Tom said, hands raised, as the man was patting down his legs. As she came into view, he broke into a broad grin. "When did that happen?" Ossana had one arm in a sling and was wearing a brace on her clearly broken nose, marring her otherwise beautiful face. The hollow beneath each eye was badly discolored.

Ossana looked down in some embarrassment at the arm in the sling. "Sparring accident."

"Who should I send the gift basket to?" Tom joked.

"Speaking of gifts," Ossana said, changing the subject, "Don't you have something for me? I don't see a bag or a case. Where is the Chronicle?"

"Not so fast, Rocky. First, I want the medicine for Edward, then you get your ridiculous Chronicle."

"Ah, best buddies now, are you? On a first-name basis already?"

"Where's the medicine?" Tom had no patience for Ossana's psychological games.

"Well, all right. You can take a quick look at it." She snapped her fingers, and one of the two flunkeys brought her a small flight case. She opened it. Inside were two steel tubes, each with a small window in the side. A clear liquid sloshed in each one. When Tom reached out, she slammed the lid shut.

"Your turn," she said. "Where's my fucking Chronicle?"

The moment had come. Could he trust Ossana to simply let him walk out of there after he handed it over? He knew he couldn't, but he had no other choice. He took out his mobile phone and tapped out a brief message, then put it back in his pocket and waited.

"What was that?"

"Patience is a virtue, sweetheart. I don't suppose you have a glass of water for me? I'm a little parched."

Tom pointed to his neck and cleared his throat demonstratively. Ossana rolled her eyes and nodded to one of her men, who disappeared in the direction of the kitchen.

Someone knocked softly at the main entrance.

"That'll be for me." Tom ignored the other guard, turned around, and strode back to the huge door. He pulled it open a short way. A young boy, perhaps ten years old, handed him a sports bag.

"*Shakar*," Tom said to the boy, and handed him the agreed-upon reward. The boy trotted away happily.

Tom spun around, a silenced gun suddenly in his hand. The first shot sent the remaining bodyguard to the floor with a hole in his leg. He dropped the flight case. The second man appeared from the kitchen just then, and

269

went down with a bullet in his knee before he had time to react.

Before Ossana could process what had just happened, Tom was pointing the pistol at her head. She looked at her men on the floor and just shook her head.

"Guns," Tom said, and the two men, groaning in pain, slid their pistols across the marble floor. "Sorry, Ossana, but I don't trust you. I'm sure you can understand why. Now bring me the case," he ordered.

Despite everything, Ossana kept her cool. She picked up the case containing the medicine and held it out to Tom.

"You could have trusted me. I had no intention of double-crossing you. A deal is a deal."

This was his opportunity. All he had to do was pull the trigger. But he hesitated, and his internal conflict was not lost on Ossana.

"Yes, you could kill me. It would be easy. But what would be the point? If I go, my father—the man who's really in charge—will hunt you to the ends of the earth. He'll kill everyone you've ever loved, and you'll get to watch before you join them."

Tom's hand trembled around the pistol's grip. A drop of sweat ran down his forehead. His trigger finger tightened slightly, then released. And again. No, he couldn't kill her. Not like this. He wasn't a cold-blooded killer like her.

Tom tossed the sports bag to her. Inside it were the three parts of the Chronicle. It landed at her feet. He reached out and took the small case from her. "You're right. A deal is a deal," he said. Ossana slowly lowered herself to her knees and opened the sports bag. "It's all there. Or don't you trust me after all?" Tom said. He lowered the gun and backed away.

As he exited the fortress, he heard Ossana turn on her guards. "What the hell am I paying you idiots for? On your feet, you useless . . ." he heard her curse as the door closed behind him.

He climbed into the waiting taxi and leaned back in the seat, happy with how the transaction had gone. Now he had to get the medicine to Edward as fast as he could.

58

QUEEN ELIZABETH HOSPITAL, CHARLTON, LONDON

"Papa!"

Hellen brightened instantly when she saw her father enter her hospital room. She had only woken up the day before, and today was the first day they would allow her visitors. Behind Edward, her mother appeared, her face a mixture of worry and hope, followed by Vittoria Arcano, carrying an enormous bouquet of flowers.

Edward and Theresia had spoken to her doctor days before. Hellen had been seriously injured, but she could count herself lucky that she had fallen at the entrance to a hospital. If the emergency team had not been on the spot, she would not have pulled through. It had literally been a matter of minutes, even seconds, between life and death. But the doctors had been able to put her parents' minds at ease: Hellen was out of the woods. In the end, she had only been in critical condition for a short time. She had stabilized quickly and then spent days in an induced coma in intensive care, under tight security. Theresia had used her UNESCO connections and asked the British government to send an SAS detachment to guard her daughter. Now Hellen had made it. She was safe.

"How are you feeling?" Theresia asked, as she and Hellen embraced. Every tiny movement seemed to cause her pain, but she gritted her teeth.

"I'm okay. It's just a scratch. I'm fit as a proverbial fiddle, as you can see." She smiled, but there was some resentment in her voice, too. She was happy to see her parents, of course. But she had counted on Tom coming, and he obviously had not. She had been looking forward to seeing François again, too. But she had a thousand questions she needed answers to, so she swept her bitter thoughts aside for now.

"Did you find anything in Italy?" she asked her father. His expression turned stony at the question.

"We managed to secure one section of the Chronicle, but it actually turned out to be in Switzerland," he said, then briefly explained what had happened. "We found the third section in the Cisterna Basilica in Istanbul, hidden in the grave of a Knight Templar—one that our Blue Shield colleagues had already inspected."

Edward looked away, his gaze roaming the room. Vittoria stared at the floor, and even her mother's expression told Hellen that something wasn't right. He looked back at his daughter in embarrassment.

"You're keeping something from me," Hellen said. Then she barely managed to ask, "What is it? Where's Tom?"

Theresia looked like she was about to say something, but then she thought better of it. She relished the idea of launching into a tirade about Tom, the man to whom Hellen had taken such a liking, though he seemed to constantly let her down. But her daughter was not in a good state, so she restrained herself and let Edward speak.

"Tom helped us find both parts of the Chronicle, the one in Istanbul and the one in Italy. And now he's vanished again—with all three parts of the Chronicle. I think he was the motorcycle thief in Avignon, and that he was working on someone else's orders. Tom's disappeared completely, and the Chronicle of the Round Table has gone with him."

An embarrassed silence descended on the room. Hellen's eyes filled with tears.

"I don't believe it. That isn't like Tom. Tom would never do anything like—"

"Well, at least there's someone here who doesn't think I'm a traitor and an asshole."

Four pairs of eyes turned to the door, where Tom was standing with his usual grin. Behind him, François Cloutard appeared, also beaming.

"The looks on your faces. Hysterical!" Tom said, making the most of their gaping mouths and amazed looks. All four were speechless. "But enough fooling around. I'm not going to keep you in suspense any longer than necessary, so I'll keep it short." He pulled a chair up beside Hellen's hospital bed and took her hand. "When I left Washington for the airport all those months ago, AF kidnapped me. I wasn't working for the CIA, and I'm sorry I couldn't tell you the truth." He took a deep breath and continued. "I was working for Noah and AF. They were blackmailing me, threatening me with all kinds of things if I didn't do what they said."

Tom looked up at Hellen's father. Edward gulped, because he could imagine perfectly well what they had used to pressure Tom. But Tom and Edward had agreed to say nothing to either Hellen or Theresia about his illness.

"Your father was right. It was me who stole the piece of the Chronicle in Avignon, too. I was tasked with finding all three sections and handing them over to Ossana. That was my job, and that's what I did."

"*You gave the Chronicle of the Round Table to AF?*"

Hellen looked at Tom in horror and withdrew her hand from his. She was the scientist again. She forgot all the danger they'd been in, everything that had happened in recent days. All that mattered was the archaeological value of the find and the fact that it was now in the hands of a terrorist organization.

Edward's glare was like ice. "I've spent half my life uncovering the secrets surrounding the King Arthur legend. The Chronicle was the best lead we had ever found, and you simply handed it over to those terrorists?" His eyes narrowed, and his expression changed from iciness to hostility. "Do you know what you've done? We're back at square one!" He sniffed angrily and Hellen could see that he was struggling.

"Oh, man . . ." Tom said with a sigh. "Do you think I'd really do that to you? Where's the trust?"

"My cue, I believe," said Cloutard, his smile as wide as Tom's. "I am not a mere extra in this scene, after all. We have officially and quite royally screwed Ossana over," Cloutard said. "Tom sent me the first part of the Chronicle through Sister Lucrezia, and while all of you were off jetting around Europe, I arranged for a duplicate to be made."

"A duplicate?" Hellen, Edward, Theresia and Vittoria exclaimed almost as one.

"*Bien sûr*. With a few small changes. You should be able to benefit at least a little from having a noted crook on your side, correct?"

The Frenchman smiled smugly and reached into his jacket, took out his flask of Louis XIII cognac, and took a swig. He held the flask out to Hellen. "A sip, *chérie*?" he offered. "To revive your spirits?"

Edward was so baffled that he completely ignored Cloutard's absurd offer to his daughter. He was still staring at Tom in disbelief. "But that . . . that means . . ." he stammered.

"That means that I handed Ossana a forgery and that AF is off looking for King Arthur's secrets at the wrong end of the world."

"The true Chronicle is safe and well in my mother's house near Siena," Cloutard added, and he treated himself to another mouthful of cognac.

"So that means we can analyze the Chronicle and keep

searching for the Arthurian artifacts?" Theresia piped up. Her nose for business had picked up a scent. "Excalibur? The Holy Grail? Tristan's love potion?" she whispered reverently.

Tom nodded. "If you can decipher all those scribbles and scratches, sure."

"Oh, don't worry about that," Hellen said, and she looked up at her father. They would work together to complete his life's dream. Together, they would finally discover all there was to know about Arthur.

A doctor entered the room then and looked at the crowd of visitors reproachfully. "Time to say goodbye and let our patient get a little rest, if you don't mind," he said flatly.

One by one, they hugged Hellen and left the room. Her embrace with Tom was by far the longest. As they went out, Tom tapped Edward on the shoulder. "I've got something for you. Follow me," he whispered.

Cloutard, in whom Tom had confided, distracted Theresia and Vittoria in the meantime with his best French charm. "*Mesdames*, may I buy you both some coffee?" he said, moving away with them. "Although I fear that the coffee we find here in the United Kingdom will be little better than dishwater."

Tom had led Edward away around a corner in the opposite direction. He pressed the small case containing the medication into his hands. Edward looked at him in confusion. Tom raised his hand and two doctors approached. "You're not going to die," was all he said. He clapped Edward on the back reassuringly before turning away, leaving Edward in the care of the two doctors.

Tom looked around. Hellen's strict physician, was gone, thank God, and the two SAS men let him pass. He opened the door to Hellen's room, and she looked up and smiled her most beautiful smile at him.

"Get well again as soon as you can, Angel. There's a lot of adventure waiting for us out there." He went to her bed, leaned down, and kissed her.

59

COUNT NIKOLAUS PALFFY'S FORMER VILLA, THE HAGUE, NETHERLANDS

SADNESS WASHED OVER KATALIN AS SHE STEPPED INTO THE house. The pain welled up inside her instantly, but she did her best to maintain her composure. She didn't want Brice to notice. Despite the difference in their ages, Nikolaus had meant a lot to her. She had not seen him as a father figure at all. She had loved him as a man and felt drawn to him in every way, more than to any other man in her life.

She had struggled with her emotions ever since they had passed the large wrought-iron gate and walked the three hundred yards along the cobblestoned driveway, lined with trees and old London streetlamps. Standing in her old home again, she could feel Palffy's presence, and it was even harder for her to keep control of herself. Everything was just as it had always been. Even in the entrance hall, the stylish, aristocratic furnishings evoked an English manor house, or perhaps a nobleman's estate from the Imperial or Royal periods of the Habsburg dynasty—not the kind of modish condo or villa so common in the luxury quarter of The Hague.

But the Welshman, too, seemed to be battling with himself. He, like Katalin, was also churning, but the emotions roiling inside him were of a very different nature. Katalin quickly made her way to the library, moving ahead to mask her emotional state from Brice. The Welshman, for his part, spent a minute or two looking around the house, calming down a little before following her into the library.

"Where's this chamber you told me about?" the Welshman asked, watching Katalin as she busied herself at a bookcase. She removed a few books from a shelf and set them on the floor. The Welshman could not see exactly what she was doing, but a moment later, she pulled part of the bookshelf forward to reveal a recess behind it. At the same time, several LED lamps around the sides of the opening lit up.

The Welshman whistled softly through his teeth and looked into the gap that had opened, about three feet wide. A ladder led straight down.

"You have to go down alone," Katalin said. "There's only room down below for one person."

In the course of his career, Berlin Brice had climbed through countless passages, crypts and caves. He was not claustrophobic in the least, but he felt a sudden touch of apprehension now. He could not explain it. His subconscious mind was going crazy, his brain calling up images from a time he had long since suppressed. But he shook it off and climbed down the ladder. Katalin was right. Down below, he could hardly move, and apart from one object—a leather folio lying on a book stand—the small chamber was completely empty. The folio was lit by a single, yellowish LED lamp.

He read the title of the large book: *Corpus Hermeticum*. It was the writings of Hermes Trismegistus, a figure representing a syncretic merging of the Greek god Hermes and the Egyptian god Thoth and who, for a long time, was thought to have actually lived in human form.

Brice opened the book.

He tilled a mighty Cup with it, and sent it down, joining a Herald to it, to whom He gave command to make this proclamation to the hearts of men:

Baptize thyself with this Cup's baptism, what heart can do so, thou that hast faith thou canst ascend to Him that hath sent down the Cup, thou that dost know for what thou didst come into being!

As many then as understood the Herald's tidings and doused themselves in Mind, became partakers in the Gnosis; and when they had received the Mind they were made perfect men.

Brice was stunned. He scanned the lines a second time. This was the earliest record of the Grail legend. And it was pre-Christian, written long before the legend surrounding the goblet used at the Last Supper came into being. The Welshman's mind raced.

Palffy had clearly given more credence to the original source of the Grail legend than most scholarship had.

And he would not have done that without reason. There had to be more to it.

Perhaps the secret of the Grail lay not only in the legends of Parsifal, King Arthur and the Knights of the Round Table, the Templar orders, or even in the tales that swirled around Mary Magdalene, he thought. Maybe the answers were to be found even further back, in the days of the ancient Egyptians and Greeks ...

Brice's heart pounded in his chest like a sledgehammer. He knew that from this moment on, his life would be devoted to one thing: the quest for the Holy Grail.

— THE END —

OF „THE CHRONICLE OF THE ROUND TABLE"

Tom Wagner will return in:

„THE CHALICE OF ETERNITY"

THE CHALICE OF ETERNITY

TURN THE PAGE AND READ THE NEXT TOM
WAGNER ADVENTURE!

CHAPTER 1
IN THE DESERT, EGYPT

With every leaden step the sturdy beast took, its feet sank into the hot desert sand. Step by step, the rider drew nearer to his destination. The midday sun blazed mercilessly down on both the rider and his trusty camel. But his dark clothes and turban offered enough protection from the relentless glare, and the dromedary plodded onward through the golden sea. The man was as exhausted as his stinking mount. Its steady motion rocked him almost to sleep...but no. He could not allow himself to give in to the urge, not yet. Not so close to his goal.

Ridwan bin Bennu had been riding through the endless dunes for three days and nights, but the ground underfoot was finally becoming firmer and stonier.

"Not far now," he said to his snuffling camel.

They would soon cross a road. He was sure of it. Just after the next hill. The information he was carrying had to find its way to the right people as soon as possible. His reward would be immense if he could get it there in time, and if he was the first.

A sandstorm just a few days earlier had taken a heavy toll on his family and his tribe. But it had also revealed a secret hidden in the desert sands for thousands of years. Now he could think of nothing except being the first and claiming the reward for the discovery for his tribe.

Finally, camel and rider reached the summit of the last ridge and there they were before him, on the horizon in the shimmering sunlight: the pyramids of Giza. It was a breathtaking sight, spoiled only by the sight of the Sodom that lay beyond. Cairo, the city on the Nile.

Three hours later, Ridwan rode past the pyramid complex. His destination was the Grand Egyptian Museum. Just over a mile from the pyramids, the new building, complementing the world-famous Egyptian Museum in Cairo, gleamed golden in the evening sunlight. Just recently, a dazzling event had taken place at the museum, making headlines around the world. In a solemn procession of specially-built vehicles, after spending more than a century in their old home, twenty-two royal Egyptian mummies— among them Ramses II —had been moved from the old museum to the new. It was an unprecedented media spectacle.

As he rode across the plaza in front of the museum, Ridwan drew amazed looks from all sides. Even in Egypt, it was unusual to see a man dressed like him riding a dromedary right up to the museum entrance. The museum was nearly complete but the grounds were still teeming with workers and engineers, modern vehicles, and construction machinery. The workers, busy cleaning up the damage done by the sandstorm, stopped what they were doing for a moment to gaze after the Bedouin.

Ridwan, who smelled no better than his animal after the journey, climbed down and tied the dromedary to a railing. Then he walked into the building through the pyramid-shaped entrance. Security stopped him immediately. Although hundreds of workers still toiled feverishly to get everything finished for the impending opening ceremony, the museum was not yet open to the public.

"I am here to speak to Husin Amin," Ridwas said loudly to the glowering guards.

"The director is not available right now," one of the security men said, wrinkling his nose and scowling.

"But it is vitally important. I must see him right away," Ridwan insisted. Draped in his dark robes from head to tough, his skin tanned almost black from the sun, he must have looked to the guards like a warrior from a bygone age. A beautifully decorated silver dagger protruded from beneath the fabric.

"Get out of here. Go! No one wants to put up with a stink like that."

A young woman, just then descending a stairway and noticing the commotion at the entrance, approached quickly.

"What's going on?" she asked sternly, pushing between Ridwan and the security guard who was manhandling the Bedouin back out the door. "It's all right. I know this man," she assured the guard, and she drew Ridwan away to one side.

Amina Yanara was the director's deputy. The Bedouin's unpleasant smell was surely not lost on her, either, but she did not let it show.

"Ridwan, what's going on? Where have you come from?"

"I have to speak to the director, most urgently."

"But he's not here. He's left for the day. What is it that's so important?"

Upset and breathing fast, Ridwan moved a few steps farther away from the guards and looked around suspiciously. Amina went with him.

"I found something in the desert, something so unbelievable they will have to rewrite the history of Egypt."

CHAPTER 2

NORTHERN SANTORINI, GREECE

"When I was a child, I loved the postcards from this place. I kept thinking it couldn't be real. Something so beautiful couldn't really exist."

From where Hellen and Tom were standing on a clifftop, they could see the town of Oia and the countless white buildings typical of the island, set against the azure blue of the sea. Hellen had laid her head on Tom's shoulder, and they gazed out together over the glittering water.

"You say that every time we come up here, and every time I think the same," Hellen said.

Tom stroked her hair softly and smiled. He'd given up counting how many times they had been to that magical spot in the last few weeks. It had become almost a daily routine for them, and it was always impressive. Every time they went there, they both realized how lucky they were. Not only because Hellen had been severely injured on their last mission and had barely managed to cheat death, but because of everything they'd been through since their chance reunion in the back of a horse-drawn *fiaker* carriage in Vienna, more than a year earlier. A lot had happened in that time, more than most people experienced in a lifetime. Tom's restlessness, his need for action and adventure, had driven him to join the Austrian Cobra unit in his twenties. But ironically, his day-to-day life in the antiterror unit had consisted mostly of crushing boredom until that fine day when he had stumbled onto an international conspiracy and met Hellen again: from one day to the next, his life had become an endless rollercoaster ride.

"We've been incredibly fortunate," Tom said.

"You're right," Hellen agreed. "Even if we haven't gotten anywhere with deciphering the Round Table Chronicle. I've been brooding over the scans every single day and I still can't make anything of the cryptic script."

In their most recent adventure, they'd stumbled onto a centuries-old brotherhood, the Society of Avalon, which considered itself the descendants of the Knights of the Round Table. And they had found scrolls written by King Arthur himself. But no one, not even Hellen or her father, could make sense of the coded manuscript.

Tom's thoughts drifted back over the last few months, recalling all they'd been through. True, his best friend had switched his allegiance to the enemy, and his uncle had certainly been killed by that same enemy—but overall the good outweighed the bad. Hellen's long-lost father had resurfaced, Tom had found a new friend and a trustworthy comrade in François Cloutard, and he and Hellen were growing closer by the day.

Tom's phone pinged. He checked the display, although he knew perfectly well what the message was going to tell him.

"François wants us back?" Hellen asked.

Tom nodded. "The usual. He says if we're not back soon, he'll feed everything he's cooked to the alley cats."

They both laughed. Since they'd arrived on the island for

their getaway, the Frenchman had made a habit of cooking for all of them every day. Including Hellen's parents, Theresia, and Edward, who had also taken a few weeks to catch their breath and were using the time to get reacquainted after so many years apart.

Tom and Hellen returned in silence to the old Suzuki Samurai that Tom had bought from a local for a few hundred euros when they had arrived on the island. It was a piece of junk, hardly worth what he'd paid for it, and every trip in it was a nail-biter. But fortunately they hardly had to drive the car anywhere. Their vacation house was situated high atop a cliff, just a short walk from the local grocery store. That was all they needed. Tom had discovered for himself that you could get by for a very long time there with two T-shirts, two pairs of swimming trunks, flip-flops, and a pair of sunglasses.

A few minutes later, they were back at the house. It was hard to imagine a place more typical of the region. It was almost kitschy. Painted completely in white, the two-story villa had a blue roof, a large terrace, and an infinity pool that made you feel you were swimming through the Aegean. On the terrace, they were welcomed by what had become a customary sight. Apart from the "best view in the world," the table was covered with delicacies, enough to feed a small army. Cloutard was pulling out all the stops. Every day he conjured an outstanding menu. It was clear that he could teach a lot of celebrity chefs around the world more than a trick or two.

After the first week, Tom had already noticed that he was putting on weight and had immediately doubled his daily run.

"I'm getting fat, François," he would say almost every day.

And Cloutard would tilt his head, point in resignation at Tom's sixpack, and shake his head. "*Mon ami*, your body is not made to ever get fat. *This* is what that looks like." And he would look down at his own little paunch and grin from ear to ear.

Theresia, Hellen's mother, was just helping Cloutard carry the last plates and bowls laden with *gemista*, *kontosouvli*, *giouvetsi*, und *moussaka* from the kitchen. All talking loudly, they sat and began to eat. Since their arrival, Cloutard had been outdoing himself culinarily every day, producing dish after outstanding dish from around the world. Today, he'd decided on Greek specialties.

"I have prepared only a single main course for today, because we have to leave soon," he said with a glance at his old pocket watch. Even in the glare and heat of Greece, the snobby Frenchman didn't change. He still looked the part with his Panama hat, walking stick, pocket watch, and the inevitable hip flask filled with the most expensive cognac in the world, Hennessy Louis XIII.

Edward looked inquiringly at his daughter. "What do we have planned?"

"Didn't François tell you? Today's the start of the Santorini Jazz Festival. The island isn't exactly over-flowing with cultural events, so we have to make the most of what there is."

Edward's expression brightened. "Of course, of course. I remember now. It's at the open-air cinema in Kamari, isn't it?"

Hellen nodded.

When they were done eating, Tom and Cloutard both jumped to their feet.

"I've got it, François. Don't worry," Tom said, taking the dishes out of Cloutard's hands. Hellen looked up in surprise and narrowed her eyes. Was Tom turning into a man who might actually be useful around the house? She shook her head in amusement.

"I'll help you," said Theresia, and she followed Tom into the kitchen.

With a sizeable stack of tableware in his hands, Tom sighed audibly when he managed to set all of it down on the big table in the middle of the kitchen without mishap.

"I've changed my mind," Theresia said, getting straight to the point. Tom looked up. He had no idea what she was talking about. "About you. I always thought of you as a selfish, irresponsible man who was only happy when he was rappelling down a wall with a gun in his hand and using other human beings for live target practice."

Tom's mind went immediately to his Cobra training exercises and he pulled a face, but he knew what she meant.

"But to my surprise, you've turned out to be more than just a mindless thug. I understand now what my daughter sees in you. Your heart's in the right place and you always try to do the right thing. You're a good man."

Tom didn't feel moved very often, but Hellen's mother had always treated him with nothing but disdain. Theresia's words meant a lot to him. He looked at the floor.

"Thank you," he whispered, barely audibly. It was all that occurred to him just then.

"When Hellen's with you, I know she's safe. And I'm also extremely grateful that you looked after Edward so well in Switzerland. I don't know what I would have done if I'd lost him a second time."

Tom thought of the crazy way events had unfolded at the headquarters of the Society of Avalon, the brotherhood that had also been after Arthur's Chronicle and the great mysteries of Arthurian mythology—the Holy Grail, Excalibur, Tristan's love potion, Merlin's fountain of youth, and who knew what else. In the past, Tom hadn't had the slightest interest in any of that old stuff. But Hellen and the de Mey family had awakened his inner history buff. Tom had even spent quite a bit of time in the last few weeks diving a little deeper into the mythology surrounding Arthur, certainly far deeper than his high school history lessons had ever taken him. But he had done so in secret, saying nothing to Hellen, Edward or Theresia.

"That won't happen," Tom said. "The Chronicle is safe now and analyzing it won't put you in any danger." He was well aware that Theresia would start worrying again the moment they returned to their dangerous everyday lives. But worrying was something that happened from time to time. She was still the president of Blue Shield, the UNESCO-linked organization for the protection of international cultural heritage. People counted on her.

"And I'm sorry I replaced you with someone else so quickly. But you'd disappeared and our team needed protection."

Tom dismissed it with a wave, signaling that it was all in the past. "Hey, it doesn't matter at—"

"Hey, you two, come back out," Hellen cried, interrupting Tom's and Theresia's talk. "Vittoria's calling from Vienna. We've got decent Internet for a change. We can even do a video call!"

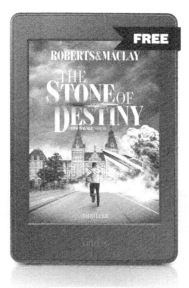

THRILLED READER REVIEWS

"Suspense and entertainment! I've read a lot of books like this one; some better, some worse. This is one of the best books in this genre I've ever read. I'm really looking forward to a good sequel. "

———

"I just couldn't put this book down. Full of surprising plot twists, humor, and action! "

———

"An explosive combination of Robert Langdon, James Bond & Indiana Jones"

———

"Good build-up of tension; I was always wondering what happens next. Toward the end, where the story gets more and more complex and constantly changes scenes, I was on the edge of my seat"

———

"Great! I read all three books in one sitting. Dan Brown better watch his back."

———

"The best thing about it is the basic premise, a story with historical background knowledge scattered throughout the book–never too much at one time and always supporting the plot"

———

"Entertaining and action-packed! The carefully thought-out story has a clear plotline, but there are a couple of unexpected twists as well. I really enjoyed it. The sections of the book are tailored to maximize the suspense, they don't waste any time with unimportant details. The chapters are short and compact–perfect for a half-hour commute or at night before turning out the lights. Recommended to all lovers of the genre and anyone interested in getting to know it better. I'll definitely read the sequel."

———

"Anyone who likes reading Dan Brown, James Rollins and Preston & Child needs to get this book."

———

"An exciting build-up, interesting and historically significant settings, surprising plot twists in the right places."

THE TOM WAGNER SERIES

THE STONE OF DESTINY

(Tom Wagner Prequel)

A dark secret of the Habsburg Empire. A treasure believed to be lost long time ago. A breathless hunt into the past.

The thriller "The Stone of Destiny" leads Tom Wagner and Hellen de Mey into the dark past of the Habsburgs and to a treasure that seems to have been lost for a long time.

The breathless hunt goes through half of Europe and the surprise at the end is not missing: A conspiracy that began in the last days of the First World War reaches up to the present day!

Free Download!
Click here or open link:
https://robertsmaclay.com/start-free

THE SACRED WEAPON

(A Tom Wagner Adventure 1)

A demonic plan. A mysterious power. An extraordinary team.

The Notre Dame fire, the theft of the Shroud of Turin and a terrorist attack on the legendary Meteora monasteries are just the beginning. Fear has gripped Europe.

Stolen relics, a mysterious power with a demonic plan and allies with questionable allegiances: Tom Wagner is in a race against time, trying to prevent a disaster that could tear Europe down to its foundations. And there's no one he can trust...

Click here or open link:
https://robertsmaclay.com/1-tw

THE LIBRARY OF THE KINGS

(A Tom Wagner Adventure 2)

Hidden wisdom. A relic of unbelievable power. A race against time.

Ancient legends, devilish plans, startling plot twists, breathtaking action and a dash of humor: *Library of the Kings* is gripping entertainment – a Hollywood blockbuster in book form.

When clues to the long-lost Library of Alexandria surface, ex-Cobra officer Tom Wagner and archaeologist Hellen de Mey aren't the only ones on the hunt for its vanished secrets. A sinister power is plotting in the background, and nothing is as it seems. And the dark secret hidden in the Library threatens all of humanity.

Click here or open link:
https://robertsmaclay.com/2-tw

————

THE INVISIBLE CITY

(A Tom Wagner Adventure 3)

A vanished civilization. A diabolical trap. A mystical treasure.

Tom Wagner, archaeologist Hellen de Mey and gentleman crook Francois Cloutard are about to embark on their first official assignment from Blue Shield – but when Tom receives an urgent call from the Vatican, things start to move quickly:

With the help of the Patriarch of the Russian Orthodox Church, they discover clues to an age-old myth: the Russian Atlantis. And a murderous race to find an ancient, long-lost relic leads them from Cuba to the Russian hinterlands.

What mystical treasure lies buried beneath Nizhny Novgorod? Who laid the evil trap? And what does it all have to do with Tom's grandfather?

Click here or open link:

———

THE GOLDEN PATH

(A Tom Wagner Adventure 4)

The greatest treasure of mankind. An international intrigue. A cruel revelation.

Now a special unit for Blue Shield, Tom and his team are on a search for the legendary El Dorado. But, as usual, things don't go as planned.

The team gets separated and is – literally – forced to fight a battle on multiple fronts: Hellen and Cloutard make discoveries that overturn the familiar story of El Dorado's gold.

Meanwhile, the President of the United States has tasked Tom with keeping a dangerous substance out of the hands of terrorists.

Click here or open link:
https://robertsmaclay.com/4-tw

———

THE CHRONICLE OF THE ROUND TABLE

(A Tom Wagner Adventure 5)

The first secret society of mankind. Artifacts of inestimable power. A race you cannot win.

The events turn upside down: Tom Wagner is missing. Hellen's father has turned up and a hot lead is waiting for the Blue Shield team: The legendary Chronicle of the Round Table.

What does the Chronicles of the Round Table of King Arthur say? Must the history around Avalon and Camelot be rewritten? Where is Tom and who is pulling the strings?

Click here or open link:
https://robertsmaclay.com/5-tw

————

THE CHALICE OF ETERNITY

(A Tom Wagner Adventure 6)

The greatest mystery in the world. False friends. All-powerful adversaries.

The Chronicle of the Round Table has been found and Tom Wagner, Hellen de Mey and François Cloutard face their greatest challenge yet: The search for the Holy Grail.

But their adventure does not lead them to the time of the Templars and the Crusades, but much further back into mankind's history. And the hunt into the past is a journey of no return. From Egypt to Vienna, from Abu Dhabi to Valencia, from Monaco to Macao, the hunt is on for the greatest myth of mankind. And in the end, there's a phenomenal surprise for everyone.

Click here or open link:

https://robertsmaclay.com/6-tw

————

THE SWORD OF REVELATION

(A Tom Wagner Adventure 7)

A false lead. A bitter truth. This time, it's all or nothing.

Hellen's mother is dying and only a miracle can save her...but for that, the team needs to locate mysterious and long-lost artifacts.

At the same time, their struggle with the terrorist organization Absolute Freedom reaches its climax: what is the group's true, diabolical plan? Who is pulling the strings behind this worldwide conspiracy?

The Sword of Revelation completes the circle: all questions are answered, all the loose ends woven into a revelation for our heroes — and for all the fans of the Tom Wagner adventures!

Click here or open link:

https://robertsmaclay.com/tw-7

ABOUT THE AUTHORS
ROBERTS & MACLAY

Roberts & Maclay have known each other for over 25 years, are good friends and have worked together on various projects.

The fact that they are now also writing thrillers together is less coincidence than fate. Talking shop about films, TV series and suspense novels has always been one of their favorite pastimes.

———

M.C. Roberts is the pen name of an successful entrepreneur and blogger. Adventure stories have always been his passion: after recording a number of superhero audiobooks on his father's old tape recorder as a six-year-old, he postponed his dream of writing novels for almost 40 years, and worked as a marketing director, editor-in-chief, DJ, opera critic, communication coach, blogger, online marketer and author of trade books...but in the end, the call of adventure was too strong to ignore.

———

R.F. Maclay is the pen name of an outstanding graphic designer and advertising filmmaker. His international career began as an electrician's apprentice, but he quickly realized that he was destined to work creatively. His family and friends were skeptical at first...but now, 20 years later, the passionate, self-taught graphic designer and filmmaker has delighted record labels, brand-name products and tech companies with his work, as well as making a name for himself as a commercial filmmaker and illustrator. He's also a walking encyclopedia of film and television series.

www.RobertsMaclay.com

Printed in Great Britain
by Amazon